TERMINAL DANGER

EXPEDITION INC. >>> BOOK TWO

J BECKETT

CONTENTS

DEDICATION

To my wife. Without her love and encouragement, I couldn't do this.

The prairie was quiet, except, of course, for the roar of arriving and departing planes several miles to the west. Denver International Airport was lighting up the sky.

The only break in the scenery was a large multi-wheeled vehicle and four black SUVs parked near a three-foot-wide hole that went underground at an angle. The faint light of a flashlight bobbed into view a few hundred feet down the sloped shaft. A dozen well-dressed men and women were standing around the tunnel mouth in a loose circle.

From inside deep inside the tunnel, a voice shouted, "Okay, we're good." A grime-covered man in coveralls crawled out.

Tom Baker had worked on a project nearby, one that he didn't think anyone knew about. He retired four years ago, moving to a small town in the mountains. His retirement had been wonderful: sipping beers on his patio, watching Interstate 70 traffic crawl by below.

Until a blonde-haired British woman approached him. She had a project she needed his expertise on, she'd said. No wasn't an acceptable answer.

He brushed his hands off on his pants, mostly moving dirt around instead of removing it. He took a deep breath and looked at the woman that so terrified him. "I was able to connect to one of the storerooms." He looked around nervously. "That's what you needed, right?"

The blonde woman stepped forward, smiling. She had approached Tom in the supermarket two months back. She was polite, well-spoken, and evil. Her blonde hair was always pulled back into a severe ponytail.

With a smile on her face, she had made it clear to him that she knew all about his previous project. She also made it abundantly clear that if he didn't help her and the organization she represented, bad things might befall him and his family down in Denver. After the threat had come the offer: more money than he ever made in a year as a construction worker. All for a few weeks' worth of work, digging a hole. The other workers on his small team were all immigrants scooped up out of Tijuana by the blonde woman. Years of construction work in the Denver metropolitan area had left Baker fluent in Spanish.

She said, "You're certain?"

Tom nodded, wiping his hands on his pants again. "Yeah. Storage room 2. Has to be."

"No alarms?"

"Nope. Like I said, they didn't go through with the project. It's all there, just not used. No security, no personnel, nothing."

"So, no one would have heard you break down the wall?"

The rest of his team, six men in dirty coveralls, were filing out of the tunnel. Tom looked around. The rest of her party was standing around impassively. "No way. No one is down there, and we're still a ways away from the airport. No one heard or felt a thing." He motioned to the men behind him. "Hand tools only, as you instructed."

"Good. Good. Thank you, Mr. Baker." She smiled and looked at the other men. "*Gracias.*"

"You—you're welcome," he stammered. "I'll just take my payment and return the—" He didn't finish the sentence or the thought behind it. In one fluid motion, the woman produced a small pistol from inside her jacket and shot Tom Baker between the eyes. Before the men behind him could react, several of the blonde woman's colleagues produced pistols of their own. Six bodies joined Tom's in the dust.

She turned to her colleagues. "Let's go. We've a radio tower to build."

PART ONE

The Key View hotel was possibly one of the most ironically named hotels that Jace had ever stayed in, further reinforcing his already dim opinion of the state of Florida.

"I hate humidity," he groused, looking out the window. Visible, barely—if you stood on a chair and looked through the corner, between the trees—was the Gulf of Mexico, and somewhere, well out of view, were the remaining Florida Keys. Most of the smaller islands in the chain had fallen to sea level rise ten years earlier. In the distance, the sky to the southeast was dark. A tropical storm was wreaking havoc on the Bahamas.

Sofia looked up from the magazine she was flipping through. "Complaining about it won't make it less humid." She reached up to run a hand through her close-cropped black hair. Even though she kept it short, it was still puffier than she liked, but now she could never admit it.

Jason turned. "It makes me feel better, though."

Sofia went back to reading. "Can you do it quietly, at least?"

Jason made a face.

Scarlet looked up from her tablet. "Children, please." She was running diagnostic on one of her projects back in San Diego.

Even though it came with the job, she hated being away from her workshop and the full computing power of Oracle, the artificial intelligence she created after dropping out of college.

Jason hitched a thumb over his shoulder. "Oracle, any update on the storm?"

From a glowing cube on the desk, the voice of Oracle said, "The National Weather Service has upgraded tropical storm Rodrigo to a hurricane. The projected path should not affect the mission, as the storm will be moving northeast to make landfall near northern Florida."

Jason nodded. "Good." He looked back out the window.

The team AI continued, "Jason, Mr. Caldwell has requested that the team meet him at the marina in thirty minutes."

Sofia looked up. "I still don't know why she's in a glowing cube."

The cube pulsed deep purple. "This is simply an interface, Sofia," the team's AI replied. "Scarlet felt that a physical representation would be, in her words, 'less creepy.'"

"She was wrong," the ex-Marine said. She put the magazine down on the coffee table.

Scarlet coughed. "You'd prefer a small animated Oracle, standing here like a video game AI?"

"Okay, no."

Oracle was housed in servers back at the office in San Diego. Their custom renovated mega yacht, the *Raven*, had a matching set of servers aboard for the AI to transfer herself to when the team was using the boat for a mission.

It was an ingenious setup. Most of Oracle could reside on multiple servers. When she wanted to be on the yacht, she needed to copy only a small portion of her code to the boat. It made life easier for everyone, especially Scarlet.

After the Canada job, Scarlet had lobbied Jason to let her leave Oracle unchained, to see what she'd learn and do in that state. Every member of the team had been wary of the AI being completely unshackled and free to do as she pleased. Scarlet had been forced to remove all the software shackles that kept the AI from full autonomy in order to help her escape the hired goons that had boarded the boat during their job in Canada.

So far, Scarlet's assurances had proven correct. The AI was every bit as helpful as before and sometimes did a good job of thinking outside the box.

For this job, there had not been time to sail from San Diego to Florida, bringing Oracle with them aboard the *Raven*. So, Scarlet had created the odd glowing cube that currently lived on the desk against the wall in the common area of their suite.

The cube was not much more than a custom-built computer with high-speed wireless internet access. By plugging it into the hardwire that the hotel provided for older computers, the AI had been able to access and take over several systems in order to better provide for the team while staying in the hotel.

Sofia thought the cube was creepy but had to admit that it did allow the sentient computer to interface with the team as efficiently as if they were in the office back home.

Jason grabbed a satchel off the back of one of the seats. "Everyone ready?"

Scarlet rotated her wheelchair, sliding the tablet into a side pocket. "All set."

"*Sí*," Sofia said, tossing the magazine on the coffee table.

The marina, like all coastal facilities over the past ten years or so, had been forced to retrofit to accommodate rising sea levels. Where the walkway structure used to slope down from the mainland to the docks below, it was now almost a flat walk from the entry gate to the docks.

In the intervening years, it had forced hundreds of marinas around the country to close, unable to make the necessary refits. This one seemed to have been built on high enough ground that it originally had a long walkway that sloped down to the water. Now, it featured a long walkway that went almost straight out to the docks.

The hired van pulled to a stop near the entryway to the docks. A worn sign proclaimed the marina to be Seaside Marina.

"Here we are," the driver announced.

"Think there's a marina anywhere that *isn't* called Seaside?" Sofia asked. No one answered.

A moment after the side door opened, the accessibility ramp unfolded, allowing Scarlet to exit the van. She looked up at the sky, dabbing her forehead. "So hot."

Jason nodded. He turned to the driver. "Thanks." The man nodded, and the van drove off.

The three of them made their way from the parking lot to the marina proper. Boats of all shapes and sizes were moored to docks that had been hastily unanchored and resecured to taller, equally hastily driven pilings.

Past the fishing trawlers and tour boats, a ship bigger than the rest, and much uglier, gently rocked.

"No," Sofia said. She turned to head back the way they came but stopped when Jason latched onto her elbow. "It's ugly," she complained.

"Well, that's just...magical," Scarlet said. The last word squeaked out, barely, before a full-body chuckle overtook her. She led the way toward the waiting vessel.

Following, Jason tilted his head. "Well, that's a thing."

Their destination looked like a floating theme park—a dilapidated, floating nightmare of a theme park painted in blue, white, and a pale goldish-yellow color. All faded. On the prow, a stylized duck in a lab coat was looking ahead with excitement. It stretched its left arm out in front of it, clutching a conical flask in triumph.

Jason led the way toward the waiting vessel. At the boarding ramp, a frumpy man in a frumpier suit, damp under the arms, motioned the team forward. "Welcome, welcome!" he boomed.

Behind him, a woman in what must be a captain's uniform smiled. "Hello. Welcome. I'm Captain Toma." She stepped to the side and extended an arm. An array of junior officers stepped to either side of the ramp.

Jason shook hands with the frumpy man, who introduced himself as Mr. Caldwell, and with the captain before leading the team up the ramp.

Captain Toma said, "We'll get underway in just a few minutes." She followed Jason and the others aboard, then headed forward.

Mr. Caldwell looked at Jason and the team. "I can show you to the operations center, if you'd like."

"Sounds good," Jason agreed, looking around the hallway they were in. Every five feet the logo of their client, a large golden circle with two smaller circles as ears, was emblazoned.

Scarlet, at the rear of the procession, a metallic cube in her lap, said, "You have the uplink I requested? Sufficient bandwidth?"

Caldwell nodded. "Oh, yes. We upgraded the communications suite aboard the *Enquiry* to your specifications."

"The *Enquiry*?" Sofia asked.

Caldwell smiled. "The *Donald's Enquiry,* to be exact." He gestured around them, taking in the science vessel. He continued, "Your requests were timely as we were planning to refurbish the *Enquiry*, and this was a good reason to move that plan forward."

Sofia tilted her head. "What else are you going to use the ship for? After this, I mean?"

The portly executive chuckled. "Well, once this job is done, Captain Toma and her crew will head south to capture the upcoming eclipse for a new feature we're working on."

"Neat," the ex-Marine replied, already looking at something else.

"And the sub?" Jason asked as the group reached an intersection, turning right and taking a set of stairs up.

"In the bay, ready to go," the other man said. "It was an interesting challenge fitting the sub into the original moon pool."

Jason nodded. When accepting this job, his team had had some very specific requests. A mini sub was one of them.

The *Donald's Enquiry* was the most luxurious science vessel Jason had ever been aboard, including the team's own converted super yacht, the *Raven*. He'd never admit that to Scarlet or the AI that controlled most of the boat's functions.

The trip from the marina to the first of the Keys wasn't a long one, but a storm out of the Caribbean was throwing a monkey wrench into the plan. Atlantic storms over the last few years had been becoming increasingly more irregular and difficult to predict.

The *Donald's Enquiry* had set sail knowing that a small tropical storm was loitering over the southern islands of the Bahamas, and by the time they reached Florida's small island chain, it had moved and grown in size and power to a minor hurricane.

"This is fun!" Scarlet shouted as the deck tilted under her chair. As a precaution, the Expedition, Inc. team and Mr. Caldwell secured themselves in the boat's operations center while Captain Toma and her crew guided the big ship through the storm. Using elastic cords, Jace and Sofia had secured Scarlet's chair in place near the central meeting table.

Across the planning table, Mr. Caldwell was looking a little green.

Sofia elbowed him. "You okay?"

He flinched, then opened his mouth to answer just as the big science vessel crested a swell, the deck feeling like it fell out from beneath them all. His mouth clamped shut as his eyes bulged.

Sofia leaned away. "Don't get any on me, *cabrón.*"

Jason cleared his throat. "Anyway. Since we've got some time to kill, let's go over the plan."

Caldwell nodded, then stopped suddenly, turning a new shade of green. He said, "As I mentioned in our initial call, we're working on a new park, one with, obviously, a water theme."

"Like Sea World?" Scarlet asked.

"No, no." Caldwell waved a hand. "More like the magical undersea kingdom of Atlantis."

"Isn't that someone else's IP?" Scarlet asked. Jason and Sofia shrugged at each other.

Again, Caldwell waved a hand. "That was just an example, and you never know." He winked. "More like an undersea adventure with a science feel, allowing guests to explore the ocean and learn about the world."

"Sounds dumb," Sofia said under her breath.

Jason glared at her. Caldwell continued, "We're pretty sure it's nothing, but given the political climate, we wanted to be certain."

"You mentioned in our earlier call finding some kind of ruins?" Jason prompted, eager to keep the briefing on task and keep the client occupied as the ship rode out the storm.

Captain Toma had assured everyone they would be skirting the edge of the storm as quickly as possible to get out of its way.

Caldwell nodded. "Yes. Several hundred meters from where we intended to set the main facility of the park. Our assumption was that as the water rose, the sediment shifted." He shrugged. "I know little about that, but know that when the Keys were evacuated, it was chaos. Beyond the occasional treasure seeker willing to risk Caribbean pirates—"

"Pirates of the Caribbean?" Scarlet interrupted, chuckling at her cleverness.

The portly executive frowned. "To our knowledge, few have ventured out here since."

Pressing on, Jason said, "Okay...According to Captain Toma, we'll be out of Rodrigo's clutches in another hour or so. Once we're over the site, we'll take the sub down, recon the area. Depending on what we find, Sofia and I will explore."

Everyone nodded their understanding of the plan.

Jason looked at Sofia. "Let's go check out the sub."

"Sweet." She rose and waved to Scarlet and Caldwell.

Scarlet turned to Caldwell. "So...You all gonna buy DC?"

"Deep Star Six, sit rep?" The voice, Scarlet's, came over the speaker in the cramped mini sub. Jason had been unimpressed when Caldwell showed them the sub. "Secondhand" was being generous.

Jace looked at Sofia, then at the ceiling. "We are not answering to that call sign."

"Spoilsport," the tinny speaker replied.

Sofia clucked. "Five by five."

As promised, Captain Toma and her crew guided the *Donald's Enquiry* out of Rodrigo's path with only some minor chop. The theme-park-owned science vessel sailed for half a day to get to the future site of the underwater amusement. Long Key was the first of Florida's archipelago to sink beneath the waves. Not the last.

The sub turned out to be less impressive than Jason or Sofia had hoped when their client agreed to provide one.

"Piece of *mierda*," Sofia hissed, slamming a palm on one of the readouts next to her. The offender blinked out, then lit back up. She fussed with the controls while Jason piloted. His low whistle brought her attention forward. "Okay, that's...creepy," Sofia whispered, leaning forward.

Through the less-than-crystal-clear bubble at the front of the small sub, the town of Layton was directly ahead.

The island had been prone to flooding during high tides and didn't last long as sea levels rose.

Sofia rubbed at a smudge of something next to her seat. "Niles might have had the right idea."

Jason clucked. "You have offers to teach at a university you forgot to tell me about?"

She made a face.

A month earlier, while prepping the site for concrete pilings to be installed for the first section of the company's new park, a construction team found ruins. Old, for sure, but beyond that, the workers did not know what it was, how old it was, or if it was valuable. Pieces of what sure looked like an ancient sailing ship.

At that distance, it was impossible to tell if silt washing away at some point, or something else, had exposed the remains of the wooden wreck. When Jason asked, no one the client spoke to could remember any wrecks off shore before the sea took the Keys. Similarly, Scarlet had found nothing online about a wreck in the area.

Something made a noise, causing Jace to look around the cramped space. The sub was a small two-person vehicle with barely enough room for two actual people. According to Caldwell, they had picked it up used from a broker that claimed it was previously owned by the Cousteau Foundation.

He looked at a patch that someone had welded in place, probably around the time Cousteau was alive. "Used submarines," he growled.

"Do you know what submarines cost?"

"Yes, that's why I made the client provide one," he replied. "I just assumed they wouldn't cheap out."

She shook her head. "They always do."

Nodding, he adjusted their course, the tiny vessel's searchlights playing across the ocean floor. "Besides, when Scar is done printing us a plane or whatever she's doing, she can print a sub."

"You say that like it's not absolutely terrifying to be inside a thing that was printed—underwater or thirty thousand feet in the air," Sofia replied. Jason shrugged. "You can't just shrug. We're not talking about a new set of miniatures for your and Niles' stupid game. You're really okay being in an airplane she made in her lab?"

"I can hear you." Scarlet's voice came over the speaker in the ceiling.

"Oops," Sofia muttered.

Scarlet continued, "It's not like the *Peregrine* is made of plastic or anything. It's steel and aluminum like any other plane. Just you wait. I've got the contractors outfitting the interior now. When we get back, you're gonna be impressed."

"Would that be before or after I die screaming?" Sofia asked.

Jace held up a hand. "Target in sight."

Outside the wide front bubble of the sub, the powerful spotlights illuminated what looked like the remains of a wooden sailing ship, possibly a Spanish galleon or barque.

"Wow," Sofia said.

Jace nodded. "Definitely looks old." He leaned forward. "Looks like we can park over there." He pointed to a section of sea floor that looked flat and stable. The mystery ship and a few bits and pieces of what might have been a dock or out-building were sitting in a silt bed, still almost half buried.

Sofia rose from her seat. "I'll get ready." She was already in a wet suit. So was Jace. She shimmied between the two seats into the small rear compartment. Jace did not know how people in bulky suits from the early '90s maneuvered around in this tiny sub but was glad wet suit technology had come a long way since then.

The pair were in suits that were as modern as could be. Thin, yet incredibly insulating. Matte black, and when not in water, designed to shed wetness quickly.

The sub didn't have a sea lock of any type. It was too small for such creature comforts. The builders designed the entire vessel to be open to the ocean. They sealed all the controls in rubber and plastic. The entire vessel functioned as a sea lock.

As Sofia donned her breather pack, she said, "Think it's real?"

Jace shrugged. "Hard to imagine it being there all this time and never being discovered, but stranger things have happened."

He guided the small craft to the ocean floor about fifty meters from the wreck. The maneuvering thrusters kicked up plumes of silt as the craft lowered toward the sea floor. With a gentle bump, the sub settled on the ground. Putting the controls into standby mode, he looked over his shoulder. "Ready?"

Sofia was slipping her helmet on. The large clear faceplate showed her smirk. She nodded. "Yup." She moved as far aft as she could to make room for Jace to suit up.

He wriggled out of his seat. "Okay, this one is a bit of a tight fit." He eased himself into a breather pack identical to Sofia's.

Their face masks were the style that covered the user's entire face, allowing for regular conversation. Jace slid his mask over his face and said, "Mic check."

"Copy," Sofia replied. She reached for a control. "Ready?" He nodded. She pulled the lever, allowing the ocean into the sub's crew space.

Scarlet pushed the control of her chair to the side, rotating. "They're going in." She smiled, though it was one hundred percent fake.

The operations center of the *Donald's Enquiry* was impressive. Scarlet hated admitting that, but it was true. It was three times the size of the ops center on the *Raven*, which made sense, given that the *Enquiry* was nearly four times the size of their custom renovated luxury yacht.

Techs in crisp white, blue, and gold uniforms worked most of the stations. Thanks to Oracle, she had hacked the ship's network and knew that most of them were monitoring Hurricane Rodrigo or prepping for their next assignment after the Expedition, Inc. team departed.

It had disappointed her when Jace took the job without enough time to sail the *Raven*, but such was life. Cruising all the way south and through the canal, then back north to

Florida, would have taken a long time. Time they wouldn't be able to bill the client for.

The upside was that she had been looking for a good field test of her ROI, or Remote Oracle Interface. The glowing cube allowed the team's AI to travel with them, despite her processing power being back in San Diego.

Mr. Caldwell rubbed his hands together. "Excellent. Once they confirm the wreck has no historic value, we can move forward with the project." He turned to look at a nearby officer. "Please let Captain know we'll be ready to return to the marina soon."

"I think you mean, *if*," Scarlet said after taking a sip of her ZapPow drink. After joining the team, she made Jason add a stocked refrigerator of the super caffeinated drink to all of their contracts.

Scarlet pointed to one of the myriad screens lining the room. "That's a good-sized wreck, Mr. Caldwell. I hope your employer has other options for their faux science lab kingdom thing." She smiled as sweetly as possible. "I wonder what it's doing there? How did it go undiscovered for so long?"

Caldwell shrugged.

The overhead speaker crackled. "We're going in." It was Jace.

Scarlet pulled a tablet from a pouch on the side of her wheelchair. Tapping an icon, she said, "Copy that. Good hunting."

The glowing cube on the edge of the workstation said, "I am receiving strong telemetry from both dive suits."

Caldwell looked at the cube, squinting. "You said that's a colleague back in San Diego?"

Scarlet nodded. "She doesn't like to travel." The cube had several wires trailing out of it, vanishing behind the workstation.

Over the speaker, Sofia said, "Damn, this thing is big. Looks old."

Jace added, "'Looks' is the right word here. Going in."

Scarlet rolled back to the station she had called hers since coming aboard.

After what the team called the Canada job, the *Raven* had needed a few weeks of dry dock time to affect repairs. Phillipe Bouchard's men had done a number on the poor boat.

As part of their making amends and mea culpa efforts, the Japanese government had footed most of the repair bill.

Jason had tried to negotiate some additional things out of the Japanese, mostly unsuccessfully. He hadn't been thrilled at the price tag for new drones to replace *Jacob* and *Edward*, not to mention upgrades to the smaller drones, *Huey*, *Dewey*, and *Louie*. The one concession he had wrung from Scarlet was to retire *Emmet*, the older drone she had used to maintain contact with the team when the more advanced *Edward* and *Jacob* had been lost at sea.

The repairs to the *Raven* had been the least of Japan's costs. The revelation of the secret base and its sinister agenda gave the country an international black eye.

The Canadians had screamed bloody murder, with the US joining the chorus. The Japanese had not tried to dissemble, owning the blemish on their honor with pluck.

That everyone involved in the wartime project was long dead, either in the base or from old age, had helped them own the crime with grace since there was no one to punish.

The policing of the bodies had fallen to the Canadian military as they led the effort to ensure the island had not been contaminated by whatever the Japanese had been concocting.

"Oh, boy," Jace said over the speaker, breaking Scarlet out of her thoughts.

Scarlet and Caldwell looked up, then to the display showing a feed from Jace's helmet cam. The view wasn't great. It was grainy and dark, even with the lights on Jace's helmet blazing.

Caldwell leaned in. "What're we looking at?"

The view shifted to Sofia, in a matching dive suit. She said, "There's nothing here." The view shifted slowly as Jace turned his head. The interior of the ship was empty.

Completely empty. There wasn't a piece of rope, or steel pulley, or remains of a single barrel. The entire hold was empty.

Caldwell looked down at Scarlet. "What's that mean?"

She shrugged. "Beats me. He's the archeologist."

"Not technically," Jace corrected from deep below the ship. "What it means, though, is that this isn't a historical find. It's a really clever recreation. Wait..." The view shifted around as Jace swam toward something.

Caldwell looked down at Scarlet. "What's he—"

"Shh." She waved a hand.

The view shifted as Jace swam around the hold. He moved to the forward section, where a staircase led to the top deck. He leaned toward the steps. "Yup. Look," Jace said. A hand, Sofia's, entered the frame, pointing to a Phillips head screw holding the step to the riser.

Scarlet held up a hand to cut off the question she knew Caldwell was about to ask. "The Phillips head screw was invented in the thirties. The 1930s."

"Oh...so." Caldwell was squinting again, his hands fluttering at his side.

"Not a relic," Sofia said over the speaker. The view from her helmet cam was showing a section of weathered hull. The weathering was fake, and in fact, now that Scarlet knew what to look for, she could see that the hull was made of composite, not oak.

"Mr. Caldwell. What happened to the other park, the one with the wizards?" Jace asked. The view shifted as he swam back toward the jagged hole in the ship's hull, Sofia on his six.

Scarlet noticed that the jagged hole was manmade—carefully, so that from a distance and even up close, if you didn't know what to look for, you'd never realize it.

Back on the *Donald's Enquiry,* Mr. Caldwell ran his fingers through what little hair he had left. "Most of the assets were sold off, or repurposed in other parks."

"Well, I think we found the ship from the pirate land," Sofia said.

"But why?" Caldwell pressed. "Surely, it wasn't always here. No park was on this Key before."

Scarlet looked over. "Guessing, to fuck with your employer." The look on the man's face made her wish she had a camera on hand. "Very Scooby Doo," she added.

Jace and Sofia left the fake wreck. "We'll be back soon." He reached for his forearm, closing the connection to the surface.

The pair swam toward the waiting sub slowly, taking in their surroundings. The Sunken Keys, previously known as the Florida Keys, were no match for sea level rise. Most were semi-preserved in the state they were when the Atlantic Ocean swallowed them.

The town they had passed over before looked like it had mostly survived the initial flooding and was now a barnacle covered ghost town.

"Undersea ghost town, that's what they should be building," he said. Sofia clucked but otherwise remained silent.

The wealthier and larger islands had been able to delay or even halt their sinking, but the smaller ones with few people didn't stand a chance. In the distance, the remains of a marina were visible, the snack bar still standing its lonesome vigil over the empty docks.

Sofia looked back at the incredibly well made mockup of what she assumed was supposed to be a Spanish galleon. "Someone really wanted to fuck with the client."

Jace chuckled. "I suspect being driven out of the theme park business, and almost going bankrupt, didn't sit well with a lot of executives."

"Rich people and their weird revenge plots."

"As long as their check clears, I don't care."

The pair reached the sub and climbed in through the

top hatch. As soon as the hatch closed, Sofia began the purge process, forcing the seawater back out of the sub, filling it with breathable oxygen.

Once the water level was low enough, they removed their helmets. The water continued to evacuate the sub as Jace climbed into the pilot's seat. "You know, if we get a new one of these, it'll have a separate sea lock." He flipped switches, bringing the sub's systems back from standby. Lights flickered on around the control board.

"I think I'm okay with just taking fewer jobs that require submarines," Sofia said, putting both helmets on short pegs at the back of the compartment. "But, hey, your money. You do you."

The sub rumbled as the small propellers spun up.

"Off we go," Jace said, guiding the vessel around the wreck one last time to get a good look at it and take photos for documentation. "I gotta admit, whoever built that thing had an incredible eye for realism and detail. Not to mention getting it here without anyone noticing."

Sofia opened her mouth, but an alert interrupted her. Instead, she uttered, "*¿Que demonios?*"

Jace was looking over the panel until he found the blinking light that was the source of the alarm. "Shit!"

"What?" Sofia leaned forward to get a look. She hadn't crawled into her seat next to him yet. She reached for the blinking light. "What's that?"

He slapped her hand. "We're losing air. Fast." He gestured to a gauge that had a needle that was rapidly moving from the right to the left. "And power," he added, pointing to another gauge.

"*Dios mio.* Cheap piece of *mierda!*" She leaned over to flip the communication gear on. "This is..." she began. She looked over to Jace. "What's this thing called?"

He frowned. "This is *Deep Star Six* declaring an emergency!"

Up on the *Donald's Enquiry,* Scarlet spun her chair and raced back to the console. "Come again? Jace, Sofia, what's wrong?" She consulted her console.

Oracle said, "I am receiving multiple alarm codes from the sub."

Three of the techs nearby began frantically consulting their stations and talking amongst themselves. Scarlet ignored them.

While Sofia wriggled into her seat, Jace said, "Power and O2 loss. Not seeing the problem." The sub shuddered, interior lights flickering. The exterior lights went dark. "We're falling to the ocean floor. We're gonna have to ditch this thing!"

Up on the *Enquiry,* one of the techs turned to Scarlet. "Ma'am, it looks like one of the power buses shorted out. It's causing faults all through the sub. The port O2 tank just purged."

"That is correct. I do not believe the situation is correctable in situ," Oracle said from her cube.

Scarlet ran a hand over her eyes.

Sofia sighed and started wriggling back out of her seat. Jace could hear her moving around behind him, getting back into her scuba gear.

"Trying to get us shallower," Jace said out loud for Sofia and the folks on the surface. The sub tilted, its maneuvering jets operating at less than half power. Two of them sputtered, providing uneven thrust. Jace flipped switches, killing the interior lights, heat, and anything else he could to help keep power to the thrusters.

Another light started flashing on the console. "Damn," Jace hissed. The ballast system was throwing an error code. With a shudder, he felt the small craft rumble as the ballast tanks opened, allowing what little air was left in the sub's systems to vent. A wall of bubbles enveloped the sub briefly.

"Hold on!" he shouted as the sub sank straight down. The lights flickered and went out.

Jason wriggled out of his seat, accepting his helmet from Sofia. "From now on, we only use new equipment," he groused.

Sofia watched him click his helmet seal, then pushed up against the hatch. It wouldn't budge. She swore, first in Spanish, then English.

Jason looked up. "Damn. Pressure differential."

Up on the surface, Scarlet looked up at Caldwell, eyebrow arched. He stammered, "We were assured that the sub had been thoroughly inspected and was in tip top shape."

"Uh huh." She turned to her screen. "Jace, Sof, what's going on? Can you evac?"

"Negative," Sofia replied.

"Yet," Jason added. He looked around the small interior. They needed to equalize the pressure, or the sub's hatch would never open.

He turned to Sofia. "Wasn't there a spear gun in here somewhere?"

She looked at him, then nodded, looking around. "I did see one...somewhere..." She snapped her fingers, or at least performed her best approximation in wetsuit gloves. She reached under the small shelf they had been keeping their breather units on, producing the speargun.

Jace accepted the weapon, tightening the power bands as much as he could. "Here goes nothing." He aimed at the glass bubble and fired. The spear flew from the gun faster than Jason or Sofia could track, striking the glass with a metallic clink.

"Did it—" Sofia started.

Something ticked, then ticked again. A crack appeared from nowhere and quickly spider-webbed the dome.

"Ye—" Jason started.

The dome shattered, and the Atlantic Ocean rushed in, smashing Jason and Sofia against the rear bulkhead of the sub.

CHAPTER 2

Misty Trenton hated days like this. Twice a month, she got a text message before her shift at the airport. She never knew when it would come and early on had lived in dread of her phone making that specific chime.

Three years ago, she had been approached by a well-dressed woman at the grocery store. She had photos and printouts of her gambling debts and credit card statements. After the divorce, her gambling problem had accelerated. She had been trying to control it on her own, and failing. Bankruptcy was on her mind when the woman approached her with the offer.

She picked up her phone and looked at the message, committing it to memory and deleting it. The messages were always the same: an origin city, a destination city, and the airline carrying the package or packages.

Sighing, she continued to get ready for work. In all the years of this arrangement, she never found out what happened to the cargo she intercepted.

"Morning, Misty," Rodrigo Martinez said as she entered the cargo facility deep beneath the main and west terminal buildings of Denver International Airport.

She nodded, taking a sip of her coffee as she went to one of the terminals, entering a search query for any manifests from Tokyo to Chicago on Oceanic AirCargo in the afternoon—the same thing she did every time she got one of those texts. After that, she went to work, like always.

While eating lunch with some of her team, her tablet beeped an alert.

"What's up?" Martinez asked around his sandwich.

Misty looked at the screen, swiping the alert away. "Nothing, just a reminder." She stood. "I'll be back."

As she walked to the employee elevator, she tapped a command on her tablet, signaling the cargo crew up on the tarmac that two crates on the Oceanic AirCargo plane they were unloading needed to be diverted for special screening.

The team lead upstairs got the alert and flagged the two crates without much thought. Hundreds of crates a day were flagged for extra screening for any number of reasons, all of which he didn't care about.

The two crates were waiting on a pallet when Misty arrived. She loaded them onto a trolley and guided it back into the elevator.

Down on sub-level two, she guided the trolley with the two crates of unknown, certainly illegal, contents to an unassuming corner of the cargo management facility. There was a door that she had never seen open, ever, tucked behind a few racks of shelving. This part of the facility was spare parts, mostly. That and crates whose labels were so worn down, she doubted anyone knew what was in them.

She deposited the two new additions and departed. She didn't know exactly what happened after she left crates at the designated location but knew that the next time she walked by, the crates would be gone without a trace. Once or twice, she saw other crates there but always assumed that was just a colleague randomly parking things there.

Either way, she didn't want to know any more than she did, and every time she made one of these deliveries, she hoped it was the last.

Niles dabbed his forehead. Even in the air-conditioned lecture hall, the heat of Phoenix was stifling. He had been lecturing in the archeology department at the University of Arizona ever since the news broke about the team's adventures in Canada six months ago.

"It turns out that the Japanese army was this close," he held up his fingers two inches apart, "to perfecting the germ weapon. If it hadn't gotten away from them, the war would have turned out considerably differently." He closed his laptop, the projection screen going dark.

Once the Canadian and US authorities finished combing through the remains of the lab on Graham Island, it was determined that the Japanese army was frighteningly close to finishing work on a germ weapon that they would have deployed against the west coast of the US with ease from the secret base. When the base went silent, the war was already turning against the axis forces. The Japanese couldn't afford the resources to investigate.

"Professor Kumalo?" a student asked. The young man had been sitting in the front row, every lecture, all semester.

"Yes, Mr. Figueroa?" he said, sliding his laptop back into his bag.

"Was the nature of the germ weapon ever discovered?"

"Unfortunately, no. When the base collapsed, it destroyed almost everything. According to the Japanese, there were no records of the base's activity anywhere outside the base."

"Almost?"

Niles grinned. "Well, as you know, my team and I could only save a few artifacts from the base in our haste to escape certain death." He shrugged. "We grabbed what we could but didn't have time to be picky."

The young man leaned forward. "Incredible. Things could have been so different."

Niles nodded. "Indeed."

"Sir?"

Niles turned to a young woman halfway up the auditorium.

"What are the Canadians going to do with the island?"

Niles tilted his head. "I don't know. The RCMP escorted my team off the island as soon as they were sure we weren't infected. We haven't been back or kept informed." He spied the head of the department at the top of the stairs leading out of the lecture hall. "If you'll excuse me, I have to go." There was a brief round of applause before the students began filing out of the auditorium.

Niles watched them all leave before heading to the top of the stairs.

"Niles." Rebecca Gilbert offered her hand. He shook it. "Great lecture. As always." Niles' lecture had filled up the moment the school had announced it.

"Thank you, Rebecca. It's been a pleasure to educate young minds again. Thank you for the opportunity."

She nodded. "It's been the university's pleasure. Your credentials have always been outstanding, and your recent adventures in Canada and the artifacts you recovered make for a truly unique opportunity for our archeology department."

Niles beamed. These past six months had been some of the most fun he'd had in ages. If he was honest with himself, he was sad to be wrapping up the engagement and heading back to San Diego and Expedition, Inc. Teaching brought him so much joy.

Smiling, Rebecca said, "Well, please consider this an open invitation any time you feel like taking the lectern. The University of Arizona system would be honored." She turned. "Come on. I'll buy you a drink to celebrate the end of the semester."

Niles grinned and followed.

Dirtbag's had been a popular hangout for university students and faculty for decades. Looking around, Niles knew Sofia would love it.

Rebecca raised a pint glass. Niles clinked his against

hers. "Cheers," she said. She took a sip, then asked, "What's next?"

Niles looked down at the table, his head shaking. "I don't know. These past six months have been, well, magical."

"Little dramatic," the woman opposite him quipped.

Niles inclined his head. "Just so. Don't get me wrong—adventuring with Jason and the others has a certain appeal, but, well, I've been shot at more times than I can count since joining Expedition, Inc. These last three months have been excitement- and bullet-free."

"Cheers to that," the dean of archeology said, raising her glass. "Our offer is still on the table." She grinned.

Scarlet guided her chair toward the table Jace and Sofia occupied. They had wrapped up the project, accepting the thanks and check from Mr. Caldwell. He didn't seem at all embarrassed or annoyed that the wreck that had delayed the project for almost three weeks was nothing more than a prop from an old theme park.

When Scarlet had pressed about the likelihood of the whole thing being intentional, the portly little executive waved a dismissive hand. You don't become a global powerhouse without making enemies. His superiors didn't care, so he didn't care.

He was less thrilled about the sub still sitting at the bottom of the ocean, but since all signs pointed to faulty equipment, he couldn't blame Jason or Sofia. He assured them he'd be speaking with the broker.

Scarlet looked at them and resumed her argument from the ride to the airport. "I'm not over this. We need reliable comms, even when not using our equipment. That was the scariest thirty minutes of my life."

Jace didn't look up from his phone. "It's not like we could surface any faster."

Sofia added, "And the sub's comms died at the same time the rest of its systems did. You were the one that routed our suit comms through the sub." She arched an eyebrow. "Also, really? Scariest thirty minutes of your life?"

Scarlet shrugged. "Okay, well, maybe the third or fourth scariest. Still." She waved a hand. "Whatever. I'm doing this. I'll redesign the gauntlets on your scuba gear to include a sat phone chip or something. I dunno yet, but this is a thing. How do you feel about trailing a comm buoy?"

Jace looked up from his phone. "What, now?" Scarlet shrugged. Jace sighed. "Looks like Niles is ready. He'll meet us at the airport." He sat his phone down on the table next to his drink.

With time to kill because Scarlet insisted on getting to airports nearly three hours before a flight, they were grabbing a bite in the food court.

Sofia sat her beer down. "I won't miss Florida. Too humid." She ran a hand through her close-cropped black hair, frizzier than either Jace or Scarlet had ever seen it.

"Hate humidity. It's like you're in a swamp, but there's no swamp."

Jace smiled. "The swamp is just the air. No arguments on the humidity."

Scarlet tilted her head. "We live in San Diego."

Jace shrugged. "It's the combo, oppressive heat and humidity. Gross." He shook his head.

The trio ate in silence for a bit. Scarlet broke the silence by saying, "Think we can get the landlord to let me keep the floating landing pad?"

Jason shrugged. "Maybe. No one else is pulling boats up, but Mr. Jaworski was pretty pissed."

Maurice Jaworski—or rather, Maurice's father—had purchased the three-building office park decades ago. Over the years, it had slid further and further into disuse, with only Expedition, Inc. occupying the park until recently.

Sofia held up a finger while she took a sip of her drink. "Actually, that one firm, the tech bros in the next building. They have a boat."

Jason nodded and sighed. "That's right. The Crypto marketing, events, and banking company, or whatever they do." The two women nodded. He said, "Well, other than them—and they'll probably go under in a year—no one else needs the space, and it makes more sense than anywhere else in the complex."

When Scarlet's pet project, her custom-designed and 3D-printed airplane, got to the point of being too big for her lab, she printed and floated a landing pad. Technically, it was a helipad, but once she scaled it up, adding appropriate buoyancy variables, it suited the plane just fine. It also took up several mooring slots in the old boat dock attached to the office park. The landlord had made disapproving noises early on but fell silent. Jason didn't say anything. He was still a little mad that Scarlet hadn't cleared her little landing pad idea with him first, but he already spoke to Mr. Jaworski about it. Agreeing to let the man use a team photo in advertisements had put the issue to bed. He was letting Scarlet worry about it a bit longer.

A gate change announcement echoed through the main terminal, cutting off whatever Scarlet was about to say. She looked up and sighed. "That's the other end of the terminal."

Jason stood up. "Let's hoof it." He collected their food trays and drinks and deposited them in the proper receptacles.

At the gate, the trio paused. Scarlet frowned, looking at the smiling older man behind an airport wheelchair, a design that had not changed since it was invented. She sighed. She patted the arm of her chair. "Bye, sweetie. I'll see you on the other side." She raised her arms.

Jace leaned down to lift her from her chair and deposit her into the wholly pathetic airport device. "Sorry, Scar."

Sofia guided the custom-designed and -built chair to the side of the jet bridge as Jace and Scar headed down the ramp to the plane. She looked at the baggage handler. "If there's a scratch on this, I'll hunt your family down, then you, then your best friend, and third-grade teacher."

The man paled. She grinned.

Nearly two kilometers east of the terminal building of Denver International Airport, small pebbles were dancing across the hard packed dirt as crews deep below worked to excavate a massive new underground expansion. The second such project in as many decades, this one was not funded by the federal government. The new facility, already several months behind schedule, would double the airport's cargo handling capacity, with some to spare. At the moment, it was nothing but a massive underground excavation project, chewing through the eastern Colorado plains about a hundred feet below the surface.

Two hundred men and women were in the Phase 1 cavern, working with boring machines, excavators, and small earth movers. The teams had been working doubles for a week, trying to catch up. The Phase 2 cavern, the final excavation, needed to be opened up and cleared by month's end in order to allow the infrastructure teams to get in and start laying the foundations for the new complex.

An earthmover rumbled over to a pile of rocks. As the driver guided the heavy machine, a sneeze he couldn't stifle overtook him. He accidentally pushed the throttle all the way forward, driving the machine into the wall at almost its top speed.

The resulting rumble didn't die down, but continued, growing louder as it did. All eyes turned to the vehicle and the wall it had struck. A section of the northern wall collapsed, nearly burying the earth mover. The driver scrambled out of the cab in the nick of time.

A dust cloud filled the entire cavern. When it settled, a

worker shouted, "Hey, boss!" He was near the site of the impact and the remains of the earthmover.

Another shouted, "Yo! Boss! JK!"

The work supervisor, JK Scheinberg, turned from the buried earthmover. "What, Jose? Mark?" He pointed at the ruined machine. "Kinda busy."

The first man, Jose, pointed. "Uh…"

JK turned. The dust from the wall collapse had cleared enough for the teams to see that where everyone expected freshly revealed cavern wall was a large hole and what looked a lot like a pile of cinder blocks. "The hell?" JK murmured, walking to the new opening. "Someone gimme a flashlight!" he shouted.

Mark came over, a pair of flashlights in his hands. "Here."

The pair played their lights around the newly exposed cavern. JK said, "Are those cinder blocks?"

Mark's beam froze. "Is that…Yo, is that a skull?"

JK moved his light, swallowing. His light froze on what looked like a femur. "Call the project manager." He turned, raising his voice. "Someone call the damn PM!" He turned to Mark. "Back away. I don't know what the hell this is, but it's above our pay scale."

Half an hour later, a ruggedized golf cart pulled up with three people: a man in a safety vest, driving, and two well-dressed women in the back.

Latricia Jackson, the airport's chief executive, and Melissa Rafferty, the cargo terminal expansion project manager, both stepped out of the cart. The former wore a bespoke business suit with pencil skirt; the latter wore a more practical pants suit that was anything but freshly pressed.

Latricia looked at JK. "What's so urgent, Mr. Scheinberg?" She had been meeting with Melissa when the frantic call had come in.

JK wiped his palms on his khakis and greeted both women. "Mel, you won't believe it without seeing it." He waved both women to follow him.

The airport's CEO checked her watch. "We have a meeting with the mayor in thirty. This had better be good."

Scheinberg clucked to himself but said nothing. He reached the opening of the wall collapse and guided the new arrivals around the beat-up earthmover.

"You dug in the wrong place?" Melissa asked. She turned to JK. "Really, man?"

"And damaged a piece of equipment," Johnson added, resting a hand on the scratched-up, yellow-painted vehicle.

JK waved the complaint away, offering her a flashlight and clicking on his own. He trained the beam into the newly opened cavern. "Look."

From over Melissa's shoulder, Latricia asked, "Is that a skull?"

Latricia looked into the dark. "Are those cinder blocks?"

JK nodded. "Yup, and yup."

"That's weird," Melissa said.

JK turned to her. "That's all you've got?"

CHAPTER 3

"Niles!" Scarlet screamed as Jason pushed her through the security area exit. She looked up. "Faster, monkey, faster!" Jason grimaced.

Niles beamed. "My dear! It's so good to see you!" He leaned down to wrap her in a bear hug. After releasing the young computer hacker, he straightened. "Jason." He moved around the wheelchair to wrap Jace in a hug. "Good to see you."

Sofia came up behind the group. "Nothing for me?"

Niles released Jason. "Always, my dear Sofia!" He wrapped her in a hug that left her toes dangling an inch from the ground.

After the hugs were completed, the quartet moved out of the flow of foot traffic. Niles said, "I'm afraid I have bad news. Our flight has been pushed back two hours. We have three hours to kill." He pointed to one of the displays mounted on the wall nearby.

"Three hours?" Scarlet groused. She looked at the unpowered chair she was trapped in. "Let's get my chair."

Jace shook his head. "They won't give it to you. It's with the checked bags." He shrugged. "Sorry, Scar, you're stuck in that for now."

"Serenity now!" she screamed, drawing several confused looks. She looked at Jason, eyebrow quirked. He sighed, moving behind the chair, taking up position to push.

Sofia looked at the others. "I could drink."

"When can you not?" Jason quipped from the safety behind Scarlet and her chair.

Ignoring him, Scarlet snapped her fingers. "Onward to the food court!"

Jace sighed and looked at Niles, who shrugged.

"So, doc, how was it? Feel good to be back in the saddle?" Sofia asked.

Niles smiled. "Indeed, my dear. It was wonderful. I wouldn't mind teaching in a place with a bit less excruciating temperatures, but such is life."

Jason leaned closer to his friend. "Scratch the itch, or...?"

Niles opened his mouth to answer, but Scarlet interrupted. "If it helps, the temps in San Diego are gonna be mild this week." She turned her head. "Oh, Sbarro!" She reached over her shoulder to slap at Jace's hand. "That way!"

"We're not eating shit pizza and baked ziti," Sofia said. She looked around. The food court in their terminal had many options, all, in her opinion, much better than mall chain pizza and pasta. She nodded toward the entrance to Marcel's. "There we go."

Everyone nodded, even Scarlet.

Over dinner, the team caught each other up on the last three months of their lives.

After the dust settled from the Canada job, Niles had leveraged every opportunity he could, with the team's blessing. First, it was a few interviews, mostly with Jason on TV shows large and small. Then, it became offers from schools to guest lecture. He had settled on the University of Arizona because it allowed him to stay in close contact with the team as needed.

With the money that Expedition, Inc. made from the few artifacts they had saved from the Japanese lab, Scarlet had upgraded the systems on the *Raven* and in the office. Oracle, the team's AI, was operating at levels her creator had never envisioned.

With Oracle's help, she had even created a version of the core system to license, one that didn't possess any of Oracle's primary functions or key systems but would outperform the smart assistants on the market by an order of magnitude.

Jason had been hesitant at first, still uneasy with the idea of artificial intelligences running rampant in people's homes. Oracle's performance in the months following the Canada job helped assuage his fears. In the end, Scarlet wore him down with assurances he'd maintain final veto power in all decisions around the licensing.

Despite its name, Marcel's was not a French restaurant. It was a burger joint.

The server came by and took everyone's order. As he left, Sofia told Niles about her time in Juarez helping families seeking asylum in the US. She'd used her cut of the Japanese base money to hire lawyers and pay for hotels. She had only come back to the states a few days before the team headed for Florida.

Niles inclined his head. "My dear Sofia, I had no idea you were such a softy."

In one swift motion, she picked up the butter knife from her bundle of utensils and jammed it into the table. "Tell no one." Niles' eyes went wide.

She shrugged. "It felt like the right thing to do."

Niles turned to Jason. "Jace?"

Jason laughed. He'd spent the time since Niles tramped off to Phoenix doing light consulting work for a startup in Seattle. The company was hoping to revolutionize underwater imaging. It hadn't been the most exciting work but paid well and kept him busy. His expertise with underwater exploration and excavation had been a big win for them.

"Well, it's not Sbarro, but this was a good choice," Scarlet said in between bites. When she ordered a plant-based burger with bacon, the server had done a double take.

Niles checked his watch after placing his empty beer glass on the table next to his empty plate. "We should head to our gate."

Scarlet looked at Jace, winked, and snapped her fingers.

The flight to San Diego was about what everyone expected of a commercial flight on a weekday. Jace and Sofia were next to an elderly woman on her way to visit family in Oceanside. She plied with them with homemade roasted nuts and stories about her son, the orthodontist.

Scarlet and Niles shared a row with a heavyset man on a business trip. He had no snacks to share but made up for it on opinions about just about everything going on in the world. Twice in the relatively short flight, Niles had taken plastic cutlery from Scarlet without their row-mate noticing.

Jace looked out the window. The towers of downtown San Diego were lit up, a view he never tired of seeing. The lights of Emerald Plaza blazed neon green, just like always.

Even with the rise in sea level and changes that had to be made to the city, San Diego persisted and thrived.

"Beautiful town. You're from here?" Ms. Santiago asked. She held out the Tupperware container, now less than half full of roasted nuts.

Jason nodded as he fished out a handful of nuts. "Yeah. Well, I was born in Chula Vista, but I moved to San Diego after college."

She grinned. "It's good you've stayed near home. Your family is here, still?"

He opened his mouth, but Sofia cut him off. "These are so good." She reached across Jason for her own handful.

The older woman replied in Spanish. Sofia beamed, and the two set off on a conversation Jason couldn't follow. He leaned back as much as he could to not obstruct them as they talked around him.

The plane bumped down onto the tarmac, smoothing out as it slowed. The pilot announced their arrival.

The moment the plane came to a stop, before the seatbelt sign turned off, Niles and Scarlet's seatmate was standing, his paunch pressing against the young hacker's face.

"Dude!" She pushed against him. He ignored her, grabbing his bag from the overhead. She turned to Niles. "I hate commercial air travel," she growled.

Jace and Sofia looked back and pointed to the front of the plane. They'd wait for Niles and Scarlet out in the jetway.

Twenty minutes later, Niles guided Scarlet off the plane. Jace and Sofia were standing next to Scarlet's chair.

She squealed and raised both arms over her head, and nodded to Jace. "Jason Kincaid, free me from this infernal contraption," she demanded with a smile.

The foursome walked and rolled out of the jetway.

Sofia waved to Ms. Santiago, who was looking at an information board. Sofia said something in Spanish and pointed toward the baggage claim. The older woman nodded and waved.

While the team enjoyed relative anonymity, there had always been a small portion of the population that knew who Expedition, Inc. was: archeology nerds, kids still inspired by Indiana Jones, ruins groupies, people that liked to stand around dig sites and watch. Sofia had a small and rabid following that no one understood and that she refused to explain.

After Canada, the otherwise abandoned office park that was their home had seen an explosion of business. Several offices were now rented by...well, Jason never really found out what the new neighbors did.

The cab navigated around the food truck corral that had appeared one day months back and hadn't left.

"Oh, look, Mad Momma's Korean BBQ is back!" Scarlet clapped as the van drove past, toward the front door of their building.

The cabbie looked in her rearview mirror. "Wait a minute." She turned. "You're them, right?"

"Please, dear. Eyes on the road," Niles scolded politely.

Heedless of his words, she pressed: "You're the folks that found that island of dead Japs and all that."

Sofia made an angry noise, but before she could correct the woman's word choice, Jason said, "Yeah, that's us." He looked up. "Here we are."

The driver looked forward; they were indeed almost to the door of the building. "That was some exciting stuff." She said to none of them in particular.

"Sure was," Jason agreed.

As the cab drove away, Sofia said, "We might need to get new identities."

Niles clucked. "Nonsense, dear. You'll adapt to fame."

He led the team to the door of their nameless building. Even after the world knew who they were, Jason had refused to put their name on the building. Even after the office park owner had offered it for free as thanks for all the new tenants he signed, Jason still refused.

Unlike every other building in the park, theirs had no security system. At least none that anyone else would recognize. In reality, Oracle watched every square inch of the building from dozens of cameras.

The front door opened automatically a moment before they reached it. From a speaker in the ceiling of the lobby, Oracle said, "Welcome home, everyone. It is good to see you."

"Hey, Oracle!" Scarlet said, wheeling past Jason and Sofia to follow Niles.

The heavyset South African man grinned. "Hello, my dear. Miss us?"

"Always, Professor Kumalo," the cheerful AI replied.

After Canada, Jason had agreed to Scarlet's pleas to leave the AI in her unrestricted form, guided only by the immutable laws of artificial intelligence as laid down by Isaac Asimov. Jason didn't really know what that meant, but Scarlet assured him it would be okay. So far, she hadn't been wrong.

He had been uneasy with the idea but couldn't argue with the results during the action on Graham Island and Oracle's subsequent self-improvement over the last few months.

Jason followed everyone as they exited the elevator into the main living space of the building. He looked at the ceiling. "Oracle, anything to report?"

"You have a message from a woman in Denver. She called yesterday inquiring about our services. Since you were traveling, I took the message rather than forward it," Oracle replied from the ceiling.

"Good call. Thank you," Jason said.

"No rest for the wicked, eh?" Niles said from the sofa where he'd just plopped down.

"So it would seem. I'll call them tomorrow," Jason said, then asked, "Anything else?"

Scarlet rolled into the room with four bottles of beer clutched in her hands, steering her chair with her elbow.

"Mr. Jaworski called again, asking about the quote he could use in his next ad for the remaining vacant suites."

Jason sighed. Sofia took two bottles from Scarlet, offering one to Jason. "Jace, he's just gonna keep annoying you. Make something up and send it over, and be done. He won't care."

"I know, it's just...Ugh. I don't want to. It's not like he's a great complex super. The sprinklers in the east lot have been flooding the planter for, like, three years."

"You don't park there. You don't even own a car," Sofia retorted.

"Jason, perhaps I could be of help?" Oracle offered. The speaker continued, "Scarlet has been working on a creative writing program for me. I believe an endorsement would be a good test of the software's capabilities."

Jason looked at the team hacker, who nodded. He said,

"Okay, sure. Give it a shot, but run it by one of us before you send it to him."

"Of course," the ceiling agreed.

"See, that wasn't that hard," chided Sofia.

Scarlet rubbed her hands together. "I'm excited to see how this goes."

Jason waved his free hand. "Whatever. I'm going to turn in. See y'all in the morning." He carried his bottle of beer back to the elevator.

Niles and the two women watched the doors close. Scarlet turned to the other two. "Bomberman?"

An hour and two rounds of beer later, the three of them turned off the large wall display. "I still think you cheat," Sofia said, stowing the game controllers in a small cubby under the display.

"How could I possibly cheat?" Scarlet asked, dropping the bottles into the recycle bin in the kitchen area.

"I don't know. You're a hacker. You have devious technology tricks up your sleeves. Not to mention your all-seeing henchbot up there." She pointed to the ceiling.

"I am not a henchbot," Oracle said.

Scarlet looked down at her shirt. Her t-shirt. "I don't have sleeves."

"Ladies, please," Niles scolded with a smile as he hefted himself off the couch.

The elevator doors opened with a ding. The ceiling speaker said, "You all should go to bed." The lights in the living area turned off.

"I shoulda made you less pushy," Scarlet said as she entered the lift, turning her chair to face the doors.

"I learned it from you," the company AI replied sweetly as the doors slid closed.

Niles and Sofia both looked down at their friend, eyebrows arched. She dutifully ignored them.

As Scarlet rolled into her room, the speaker in the center of the ceiling said, "Scarlet, I have been meaning to speak to you regarding the *Peregrine*."

Scarlet went about her nightly routine as she talked to the intelligent management system for the company's assets. "What's up?"

"The contractors departed yesterday afternoon. I was able to inspect their work via the *Peregrine*'s onboard cameras and one of the smaller drone units. I believe the plane is ready for her first flight."

"That's great. Throw the latest diagnostic up on my screen, please." She rolled into the restroom. There weren't any cameras in any of the team's rooms, but she still closed the door.

Jason had spared no expense when outfitting the building for the team to live in. He figured it'd be easier if everyone was under one roof. With enough space to not feel like they were on top of each other, it mostly worked.

Sofia had a place she sometimes retreated to when being around everyone got to be too much. No one knew where it was, despite repeated asks. Scarlet had even attempted to have one of her pet drones follow the ex-Marine. Sofia shooting the drone down had put an end to any further attempts to find her hideout.

After Scarlet finished in the restroom, she parked in

front of her desk, the latest diagnostic data waiting on the screen.

The *Peregrine* had started as a pet project, mostly to see if she could, in fact, design and build an aircraft. Once she saw that she could, then it became a project to build the best, most advanced aircraft possible. The team couldn't travel by boat for every job, as Florida had just proven. The more she could keep them from flying commercial, the better. Mostly for herself, since every single commercial flight was an indignity.

The industrial fabrication system she had in her lab building by the marina had been working overtime since then to build the *Peregrine*.

By the time the team left for Florida, the entire airframe and exterior were complete, assembled, and moved to the floating landing pad she constructed beforehand. The landing pad had the added benefit of not requiring strangers to have access to her lab building. All teams arrived and worked without entering any Expedition, Inc. spaces, which kept Jason happy.

Once the construction was complete, Scarlet hired contractors to outfit the plane with actual passenger accouterments. Oracle had overseen the work, remotely using the array of cameras on the plane attached to the nearby building and a few small, mostly quiet, drones.

Scarlet stifled a yawn. "Do you have a drone charged?"

"Of course."

"Launch it and pipe the video through. I want to check it over."

The screen updated to show the view from a small

quad copter drone as it made a slow pass down the length of the compact craft, first fore to aft, then along the opposite side and back toward the cockpit.

"She's beautiful," Scarlet whispered.

JK Scheinberg had only been to Latricia Jackson's office once before, when he came on as supervisor for the project, after she fired the last manager. As far as he could remember, that was the only time he had spoken more than a few words, usually hellos or goodbyes, to the woman. She was busy running the country's second busiest airport, after all.

She had held the position for three years before the expansion project started, and by all accounts, the mayor and city council liked the results. When she pitched the cargo depot expansion, the city had rallied to find the funding.

Melissa Rafferty, on the other hand...He met with her at least once a day, usually in the morning before he headed down into the work site.

She came from a software background, so daily stand-up meetings were her thing. It had taken him a while to get used to them, but now, he enjoyed the daily briefings.

Latricia looked up from the tablet she was holding. "Okay, so what the fuck do we do about this..." She waved her hands. "...Thing, tunnel, graveyard, whatever?"

JK raised his hand. "I don't think it's a burial ground. It

was only the one skull." The look he got made him take a step back.

Melissa blew out a loud breath. "We could send a team in?"

JK looked at her. "Of what? My guys? They don't know what that thing is. They'd likely get themselves killed in a cave-in or something. Or possessed by angry spirits."

"You said it probably wasn't a burial site," Latricia pointed out.

He sighed. "Whatever. Plus, that for sure ain't in our contracts."

Melissa looked around the room. "What about Clark's people?" JK and Latricia turned to her. "They're security trained, after all."

JK shook his head. "They're paramilitary rent-a-cops."

Ignoring JK, Latricia nodded slowly. "That makes sense. We can at least have them take a look." She reached for the phone on her desk, pressing a button.

A moment later, a man said, "Go head, ma'am."

"Clark, can you come up to my office, please?"

"Be right there."

"While we wait..." Melissa said. "What did the mayor say?"

The darker skinned woman behind the desk clucked. "She was...not thrilled."

The office door opened, admitting a well-muscled man in his early fifties. "You wanted to see me?" Latricia waved him in. Spying the other two members of the meeting, he nodded. "Melissa, JK."

"Hey, Clark," came back in unison.

The big man took up position next to the other two. He was in his usual uniform, black with blue highlights. His salt and pepper hair was in a tight buzz cut.

Latricia cleared her throat. "Clark, we've got a…situation."

"The tunnel," he offered.

Melissa and JK traded a look.

Latricia nodded. "I guess it's not as secret as we hoped."

The bulky man shrugged. "It's my job to know things. So, what? You want me to send a team in? Clear the tunnel? Demolish it?"

Melissa raised her hand. "More like just take a look. The tunnel seems to head deeper under the airport and off toward the plains. We need to know more about it. Who built it? Why? Where does it end in both directions? That sort of thing."

Clark smiled. "We'll take care of it." He looked around the room. "Anything else?"

"No. Thanks, Clark," Latricia replied. He nodded and left.

As the door closed, JK looked at the two women. "He freaks me out."

With sea level rise, the world's war on terror had shifted from airports and the Middle East to the thousands of miles of coastline that the developed world had ignored for decades. The navies of the world were unequipped to deal with the threat of hundreds of small, often scratch-built and repurposed, vessels showing up in sovereign waters all over the place.

For America, that mean that the Coast Guard suddenly found themselves in the center of everything.

The Transportation Security Administration was the big loser in the massive reshuffling of military spending. Airports were deemed as safe as they had ever been, so TSA budgets were cut nationwide.

Airports, having become dependent on the TSA over the years, were left in a lurch.

Many, like Denver, hired private security firms to pick up the slack. TSA still managed the actual checkpoints and screening areas, but that was it. All other security concerns were left to security contractors.

Steel Palisade Security had been Denver's choice. The firm had hired several TSA agents over the years with more joining daily after the reduction in funding. That allowed for a nearly seamless transition.

In no time, SPS was securing the airport inside and out.

Ever since SPS had been hired, petty crime had dropped and serious crime had all but ended anywhere near the airport. Complaints of aggressive behavior had risen, but for the time being, Latricia was happy with the ratio so let things remain as they were.

CHAPTER 4

Clark Haggerty left the executive offices section of the administrative building and headed for the section that SPS had taken over for their onsite operations.

Haggerty had been with SPS for ten years, recruited right out of the Marines after the invasion of the Philippines.

An alliance between the United States, Australia, and Japan had engaged in an effort to stamp out a rogue regime that had taken over the archipelago.

The effort had been a complete failure and international embarrassment. Senior military leaders from every nation had been given their walking papers, including Sergeant Major Clark Haggerty.

Private security firms were always looking to poach people with military experience. Clark had been home and unemployed for less than three days when a representative from SPS had approached him.

They had been looking into opening a new office in Denver and needed someone with leadership skills to run things. The Denver office was up and running for only a year when the shake-up with the TSA and Coast Guard occurred.

After closing the deal with Denver International Airport, SPS had locked in Colorado Springs and several smaller regional facilities across the Rocky Mountain region.

Under Clark's leadership, SPS took a militaristic approach to securing their client facilities. While it worked, it wasn't without casualties. SPS ran the airport like a military base.

The SPS operations room was busy. Several officers were watching live feeds from hundreds of cameras around the multiple terminals and employee-only areas of the airport.

The new construction project was a black spot in the SPS surveillance operation, but scuttlebutt travels fast. Whatever was down there, it was causing disarray. Disarray would only spread and cause further instability. He had spent too long getting things just right at this airport to let some weird tunnel fuck it up.

"Get a team together," he barked, then added, "Make it two!"

"Finally!" Scarlet burst, as Sofia exited the elevator and walked into the kitchen space on the second floor.

Running a hand through her close-cropped black hair, the ex-Marine said, "What's wrong, *chica?*"

Jason held out a hand in front of the excited hacker. "Her new toy is ready for a test run, and I told her she needed to wait for you." As impressed as Jason was that Scarlet had built an airplane, he wasn't about to let her take it up on her own.

"Why do I have to be with her when she crashes to the ground in a fireball? I don't wanna die."

From the table, a bowl of oatmeal in front of him, Niles said, "Because I already said no." He didn't look up.

Jason clucked. "He did, but also, you have flight training."

"Come on, Sof! It'll be fun and perfectly safe. I've been taking online flying lessons and running simulations for days."

"A flight simulator game is not *lessons,*" the other woman retorted. She turned to Jason. "Jace, come on. You have had flight training, too." She turned to Scarlet. "Jace?"

Jason quirked an eyebrow. "I said no before he did." He inclined his head toward Niles.

After releasing an explosive sigh, Sofia relented. "Fine." She grabbed a travel mug and filled it with coffee. "Let's get this over with." She looked at the two men. "I was going to clean the gym this morning. Guess one of you can do that." She winked.

As the two women boarded the elevator, Jason looked at the ceiling. "Oracle, can you connect me with whomever it was that called us from Denver? I'll head to my office in a second."

"Of course, Jason," the ceiling speaker replied.

He turned to Niles. "Want to join me?"

The other man hefted himself up from the chair. "Sure."

Asking permission was never Scarlet's strong suit. When she assembled and floated her upscaled helipad, Mr. Jaworski hadn't been thrilled. When he saw it was a plane she planned to land, his mood hadn't improved.

"Okay, this is cooler than I expected," Sofia said as they approached the craft. The pad bobbed gently in the marina, a dozen yards from the *Raven*.

Though it had started out more airplane-like in design, Scarlet made modifications as she went until the *Peregrine* resembled something from a science fiction movie.

Instead of narrow back-swept aerodynamic wings, the craft sported stubby wings that ran three quarters the length of the craft, forming wide triangles. Mounted on the end of each wing was a jet engine that would be at home on a much larger craft. The entire plane was matte black.

"Why black?" Sofia asked.

"Radar absorbing paint." Scarlet shrugged. "Only comes in one color." Sofia barked a laugh as Scarlet guided them to the rear. "Oracle, open her up, please."

Something in the craft made a clunk as bolts slid out of position. A heavy ramp in the craft's aft end descended to the ground.

Unlike most commercial aircraft that sat on three tall landing gears that put the craft nearly five feet off the ground, the *Peregrine* sat low to the ground on four squat landing wheels, barely a foot off the tarmac.

Sofia cocked her head, unsure how anyone would service the craft with it sitting so low to the ground. She shrugged; not her problem to solve. She said, "Wait a minute. This thing looks a lot like that ship from the show you love."

Scarlet grinned. "There's a passing resemblance. Always a brown coat." She winked as she rolled up onto the ramp.

"Welcome aboard, Scarlet, Sofia," Oracle said from an overhead speaker.

"Ready for a test flight?" Scarlet asked, rolling down a corridor wide enough for her chair and a person to cross paths. No crappy commercial airline wheelchairs here.

"I am. I have completed all standard pre-flight checks and am awaiting sign-off."

Sofia tapped her friend's shoulder. "She's gonna fly?"

Scarlet nodded. "Yup. Well, that's the plan, at least. She's been absorbing flight data, sims, logs, and anything else I've been able to find and upload to her for a few months now."

"Please rest assured, Sofia. All flight systems must be attended by a human, even when I am in control. Just in case."

The pair moved down the corridor, passing two equipment bays, then a bunk room and head opposite each other. The corridor opened into a wide lounge space with a sofa and chair, a small pantry, and a workstation. Directly ahead was a wider pocket door that looked reinforced.

Sofia pointed. "Cockpit?"

Scarlet nodded. "Yup. Figured I'd bulk up the security,

just in case." The doors slid apart to reveal the spacious-for-a-cockpit, cockpit. Scarlet whistled. "Those contractors did an outstanding job!" She ran a hand along the back of a seat. "Leather?"

"Corinthian." Scarlet chuckled.

"That's not a thing," Sofia protested.

The pilot station had more room than any pilot had a right to. It sat directly in the center of the wrap-around forward windscreen. Directly behind it were two stations, one on each bulkhead.

"No co-pilot?" Sofia asked.

The ceiling answered, "Technically, the pilot station is the co-pilot."

Sofia grinned. "Someone is full of themselves."

"Hate the game, not the player," the ceiling replied. Sofia turned on her friend, who shrugged.

"We have been given clearance to lift off," Oracle said. The AI added, "San Diego International has requested we observe altitude and airspace restrictions."

Sofia was in the pilot's seat. "Copy that." She had spent a few minutes familiarizing herself with the controls before telling Scarlet and the AI that they could request takeoff clearance. They had moved the *Peregrine* to the small office complex's helipad. Long before Jason had moved in, there was a medical research firm two buildings over. They had paid to install and license the helipad, then moved a year later.

"Finally," the hacker said from the station she had designed for only her use. There was no chair. Instead, it had specially designed clamps that could lock her chair into position. Several monitors showed the plane's various systems. She had been absentmindedly drumming her fingers as she and Sofia worked through a myriad of pre-flight lists.

Sofia clucked. "We don't rush things when crashing into a mountain is a possibility." Behind her, Scarlet made a face. "I saw that." She looked at the various digital gauges. "Okay, Oracle, do your thing."

"Very good," the AI said. Something whirred and clicked, and even though Sofia couldn't see them, two louvred ducts slid open near the wing roots opposite the craft's center of gravity. Each of the four vents could adjust independently, fed by the massive jet turbine engines at the end of the wings.

The engines spun up with an electric whine. Sofia turned to look over her shoulder.

Scarlet winked. "Electric. Most of the cargo space below deck is batteries. We're heavier than a plane our size, but hey, we can charge anywhere that has 220."

"Like a parking lot?" Sofia quipped.

The *Peregrine* rose off the ground and teetered briefly as Oracle processed millions of bits of data to balance the craft on the thrust from the four wide open vents. The two large engines roared as they increased power, providing forward thrust.

The *Peregrine* moved forward, first at a slow drift as the VTOL vents angled to provide additional forward thrust. As the engines reached full power, the internal valves that sent thrust to the VTOL system began diverting power to the main engine thrust nozzles. As the aircraft picked up speed, the VTOL vents slid closed, sealing the wings and forming a seamless aerodynamic surface.

"Off we go!" whooped Scarlet as the matte black craft shot into the sky.

Sofia watched the console for a minute before looking out the forward windscreen. "Okay, this worked out better than I expected."

"I do not know if I should be offended," Oracle said.

"You should," Scarlet said, then added, "I am." She turned to Sofia. "I'll have you know that this is the 207th—"

"Ninth," Oracle interrupted.

"—Ninth iteration of this design," Scarlet continued. "Oracle and I crashed thousands of times to come up with this design. It's—"

"Do. Not. Say it." Sofia held up a finger.

Scarlet sighed. "Superstitions, bah." She turned her attention back to her station. "Oracle, are you seeing the power flow variance between port and starboard?"

"I am. I have logged it on the to-do list and made the necessary adjustments to the engines to mitigate the issue for the time being."

The *Peregrine* was flying out over the Pacific Ocean when the entire craft shuddered. Both women looked at each other, then at their respective consoles. The craft shook again, harder.

"Warning, port engine experiencing nonstandard power consumption."

The craft lurched to the right as the left engine spun up its output. The power reading on Sofia's console moved into the red.

"What the hell is going on?" Sofia demanded. She reached for the manual controls. "Oracle, manual control."

"Unable to comply," the AI replied.

Sofia spun to glare at Scarlet, who shook her head and turned. She was furiously tapping on the keyboard before her.

"If we die, I'll haunt your family forever," Sofia said. Her hands were on the manual controls, even though they remained locked out.

Outside the cockpit, the sky suddenly shifted up, as the ocean came into view.

"We're not going to die. Probably," Scarlet said. The whine of engines faded to nothing. The silence that followed was off-putting, to say the least.

"Scar—" Sofia began but stopped as the sound of the engines spinning up blared through the craft. She hadn't released the manual controls, and suddenly they jerked in her hands. Her entire attention snapped forward.

"Engine restart complete," Oracle announced. "All engines responding and reporting nominal power flow. Batteries at 78 percent."

Scarlet released an explosive breath. "See, not dead." Sofia turned just enough to glare.

Scarlet pulled a face and turned back to her console. Under her breath, she said, "Oracle, what happened?"

"I believe the power imbalance we discussed previously was more severe than my initial diagnostics were able to determine. The compensation I implemented was a miscalculation. The resulting imbalance fed back into the central power bus, which—"

"Okay. Got it," Scarlet interrupted. "Put the entire power system on the list."

"Already done."

The rest of the *Peregrine*'s test flight was far less exciting. After convincing the flight controllers at San Diego International Airport that they weren't in trouble, Scarlet instructed Oracle to put the small craft through its paces, which she did under the watchful eye of Sofia, who never once released her grip on the flight controls.

Sofia's initial distrust waned as the *Peregrine* performed maneuvers that the average private jet could never match, some that even the latest military aircraft would struggle to keep up with.

The two oversized engines pushed the plane to speeds that would require some explaining, eventually. The VTOL system was able to slide open and activate in less than ten seconds, allowing the craft to go from cruising speed to a slow, steady hover before passengers would feel their stomachs lurch.

Walking back into the main building, Sofia said, "So, we just park it on that floating pad now?"

Scarlet was staring intently at her tablet as she guided

her chair into the building. Without looking up, she said, "Yeah, Mr. Jaworski wasn't thrilled, but he hasn't mentioned it in a while, so," she shrugged, "maybe he got over it."

"Having famous tenants helps," Sofia quipped.

"Ladies," Niles said, meeting them as they exited the elevator. "I was just getting ready to head out on a shopping run and was hoping Sofia would join me."

"Are you still afraid of the Wharf Mall?" Scarlet teased.

The older man flushed, his skin darkening several shades. "My dear, that salesman was downright hostile and aggressive. I was there for an hour." He raised his wrist to show them his watch. "And I'm still paying off this thing!"

"Why do you wear it?" Scarlet wondered.

Niles clucked. "It cost a fortune."

Sofia chuckled. "Come on, old man." She turned to Scarlet. "Have fun debugging your airplane or whatever."

Scarlet waved her tablet. "You said that to be mean, but Oracle and I are going to have an absolute blast." She guided her chair back into the open elevator. Her workshop was better than any of the terminals Jason had installed in the common areas of the building.

The Wharf Mall was a fifteen-minute ride from the office park. As Niles offered his hand to Sofia, exiting the rideshare vehicle, he looked around. The mall had been built into the remains of a failed addition to the convention center.

When the water rose, the lower level of the center flooded. A developer had purchased the building from the city, choosing to make a mall out of the level still above water. The submerged level was reinforced and closed off.

The closing-off part hadn't stuck. The less desirable elements of the city's population had taken up residence in what they called the shallows. No one seemed to mind so long as the denizens of the shallows didn't cause trouble for the mall's shoppers.

Unlike malls from Niles and Sophia's childhoods, the Wharf Mall was more indoor swap meet mixed with a strip mall. Throw in an active trade in illicit wares, and that was the Wharf Mall.

The mall's owner arranged the mall in a grid of sorts. The only entry into it opened on the center aisle, which was a bit wider than the others and home to the vendors who could pay higher rent. You could get the latest techno gadget from one vendor and fresh produce from the state's agricultural center at the next. There was a vendor, or two, for anything you might want at the Wharf Mall.

Delicacies from Eastern Europe had an entire row to themselves. Another row catered exclusively to goods from the parts of South Africa still above water. Not to mention the military surplus from more than one military—Sofia's favorite section.

Sofia loved it. Niles tolerated it. It was the nearest location from which to stock up for missions but also do basic grocery and necessities shopping. That Niles was such an easy mark for the various hucksters caused Sofia no end of pleasure. Whenever he managed to let himself get snagged, she'd watch him suffer, then swoop in and save him.

Niles headed for the consumables section. "We need to stock the building's larders."

"Larders?"

Niles clucked. "Buy a thesaurus, my dear."

She clucked but fell in beside him as he guided a small cart between people.

They were just filling a cart when Sofia's phone rang. She looked at it. "Jace," she said to Niles. She tapped the icon and held the phone to her ear. "What's up, boss?" She listened for a bit. "*Sí*, so just mission food? *Sí...sí.*" She looked at Niles, smiling. "*Sí.* We'll be back in a bit."

Niles watched her slip the phone into her back pocket before saying, "Took the Denver gig, I take it?"

She nodded, removing a few things from the cart and placing them back on the shelf. "No need to stock the larders." She winked. "But we do need Cheetos."

He removed his own phone from the black patent leather hip bag he wore, to the chagrin of the others, whenever they were home. He scrolled and tapped a bit. "As interesting as Denver sounds, I hope it doesn't take too long. The University of Wisconsin has an open guest lecture spot a month from now."

"*Ay*, Wisconsin? So cold," the Hispanic ex-Marine said. "Why you want to go there?"

He zipped his belt pack closed. "One rebuilds their career when and where they can, my dear." He turned and pointed to the sign for dry goods and camping equipment. "Not all of us are cut out for being shot at and having ancient ruins fall on our heads." He hustled off, doing his best to avoid the vendor with luxury watches on display at the end of the row.

"Team 2, move in," Clark said into his handheld radio deep beneath the airport, in the cavern of Phase 1 of the baggage and cargo expansion.

On the screen of the tablet he held in his other hand, six men and women, armed with pistols and flashlights, entered the newly discovered tunnel and turned east, the direction away from the airport.

Team 1 had entered ten minutes earlier, heading west, back toward the airport only to hit a cinder block wall half a mile in, roughly where the west terminal was originally slated to be located. During construction, the bulk of the below-ground facility had to be shifted half a kilometer from the original plans. There wasn't any sign that anyone had used the tunnel in that direction since it was dug.

The tablet screen was split into six views from each of the team's chest-mounted cameras.

"This is weird," one operator said. "This isn't natural."

"What gave it away?" another asked. "Was it the cinder blocks or the old wiring and Edison bulbs?"

"Shut up, Hicks. Asshole."

"Can the chatter, people," Haggerty scolded. Most of them he had handpicked, but a few had been brought on while he was supervising a job in the Amazon and been out of reach. "We've got a job to do and the sooner—" A loud pop and screaming interrupted him. The ground shook.

"Fuck! What was that?" someone behind Haggerty shouted.

On Haggerty's screen, one of the six squares was static. The others were a jumble of incomprehensible images. "Report."

"Where's Drake?" someone in the tunnel shouted.

"I think he was to the right," another voice answered.

The views on the tablet were moving back and forth, the members of the team slowly calming. Flashlight beams illuminated people and sections of wall at random.

"Report, goddamnit," Haggerty growled.

"Sorry, sir. A section of the wall exploded. Drake is down hard. Dietrich looks concussed. The tunnel is half collapsed."

"What happened?" the burly mercenary demanded.

"There must have been a booby trap. I don't know. One minute we were walking, and the next, the tunnel wall exploded."

"Can you proceed? Send Dietrich back and continue?"

"I think so."

"Do it."

On the tablet, the confusion had died down, replaced with five orderly views of the tunnel. Four were moving together, west. One was returning to the Phase 1 cavern.

Haggerty looked around. "Get a med team. We need to retrieve Drake."

Someone acknowledged.

Ten minutes later, one of the mercenaries said, "Not seeing any more booby traps."

"Stay sharp. One means there's many," the security chief said.

"Copy that," one of the remaining mercs replied.

"I don't think anyone has been down here in a while. Lot of dust and shit down here."

"No more bones, at least," one of the team members quipped.

Haggerty looked up as Dietrich came back into the cavern. Another member of Haggerty's crew met her. He was about to ask a question when one of the team on the tablet display said, "All stop." The view from her camera angled down to look at a section of the floor, her flashlight highlighting a thin filament that entered a hole drilled in the cinder block at the base of the wall.

Whoever had rigged the place had been a pro. With the explosive inside the concrete block, disarming would be next to impossible.

Over Clark's shoulder, a voice said, "Bring 'em back."

He turned. "This is what we're paid to do, Rafferty," he replied.

"You're paid to keep crime down and keep the airport safe. This..." She pointed at his tablet screen, then to the stunned Dietrich on a bench against the wall. "...Is not that. Our contract with your firm has rather aggressive payouts for casualties and fatalities. You've already got one dead and one injured." She put a hand on his shoulder. "No offense. This isn't your area of expertise." When he glared at her, she pressed. "Can any of your people even spell archeology? This is clearly some type of ruin or facility no one knew about. It's not a security issue."

He growled and held up his radio. "Fall back. I repeat, fall back." He turned to one of his officers. "Get a drone."

A pair of SPS officers emerged from the tunnel, a stretcher between them, Drake's body on it.

"Okay, team." Jason clapped his hands as he stepped off the elevator into the living space of their building. "Got a gig." All eyes turned toward him.

"Already?" Scarlet said, putting down the tablet she was looking at.

"The thing in Denver," Niles offered.

Jason nodded. "A construction project under the airport found an old tunnel."

"A tunnel?" Sofia said from the couch where she was reading a romance novel, a not-at-all-guilty pleasure of hers. She closed the reading app on her tablet and looked up.

"What kind of construction project?" Scarlet asked.

Jason nodded again. "They're expanding the cargo terminal, mostly underground. Apparently, Denver

International Airport is doing good business as a cargo hub and needs more capacity." He looked at Sofia. "Tunnels of the old-but-not-too-old variety." He snapped his fingers. "And they're booby-trapped."

"Booby-trapped?" Scarlet repeated.

"That's what I said." He moved to join Niles at the dining table, motioning for the others to join.

Niles cleared his throat. "Indeed. The woman in Denver mentioned that the in-house security contractor has already lost one person."

Rising from the sofa, Sofia asked, "Lost a man?"

Jason nodded. "Apparently, there was at least one booby trap. A team went in to see where the tunnel went, didn't spot the trigger, and," he spread his hands, "boom."

"Yikes," the ex-Marine said.

"Boom?" Scarlet repeated.

Sofia frowned. "Ruins?"

Jason shook his head. "Hard to imagine."

Niles nodded his agreement. "The indigenous peoples of that area weren't tunnel- or mound-builders." He rubbed his chin. "There were cliff-dwellers, however, but they were in the southern parts of the state, so..."

Sofia detoured to the fridge, grabbing a fresh beer for herself, and three more for the others. Jason looked at her, then pointedly at his watch. She said, "You didn't almost crash into the ocean." He tilted his head. "Or have to go shopping with Niles."

Jason turned to Scarlet, who said, "Technically, you didn't either, you big baby." She turned to Jason. "There was a minor technical difficulty, but it's fixed now. That's why we do test flights."

Jason accepted a beer from Sofia, his eyes on Scarlet. "Will it get us to Denver?"

"No." Sofia took a sip.

"Yes." Scarlet glared at the other woman as she accepted a beer. She looked at the ceiling. "Right, Oracle?"

"That is correct. The issue we experienced earlier today will not reoccur," the ceiling speaker nearest the dining area replied.

"Oh, good, we can try a new error," Sofia retorted.

Jason sighed. "Ladies..."

Oracle replied first. "Since landing, I have run 478 simulations with the data I collected today. I have encountered zero issues."

Scarlet stuck her tongue out at Sofia.

Niles watched the two women. Scarlet turned from Sofia and said, "If I recall, they want us to check out the tunnel."

After taking a sip of his beer, Jason nodded. "Yup. Like Niles said, they lost a security man to a booby-trap. The exploding kind. It almost caved in the tunnel. Another officer took a chunk of concrete to the head. That was more than enough for the project manager to pull the plug and call in the experts. Us."

"So, they don't know where it goes?" Scarlet asked. She was already thinking about the ways to load one of her larger drones from the *Raven* into the *Peregrine*.

Jason dashed her hopes by saying, "They sent a drone in. It found a door almost a kilometer in. Old. Steel. Visibly locked. The PM and airport CEO both agreed that the scope of the mystery was outside the skill set of the rental mercs they use for security."

Niles rubbed his palms together. "Hence, us."

Jason nodded.

Scarlet ran a hand across her face. "Interesting. No plans on record?"

Jason shook his head. "None. As far as the airport folks know, where they're digging should be prairie dog burrows and rocks."

"I swear to God, better not be another secret Japanese base," Sofia said with a smirk.

Niles chuckled. "What are they hoping for us to do? The woman this morning didn't say."

Jason inclined his head. "They're hoping it's nothing more than an old undocumented bomb shelter or something that someone dug during the war."

Sofia said, "I was reading an article in Forbes last week, maybe the week before. Denver's economy has fully rebounded, and they're seeing two to three times month-over-month growth in traffic at the airport." Jason and Niles both turned to stare at her. She shrugged. "What?"

Scarlet produced another tablet from somewhere and, without looking up, said, "Where's the tunnel go? I mean, the other end?" She had a satellite view of Denver International Airport on the screen. She was panning and zooming.

"According to Ms. Rafferty, the near end of the tunnel stops where the old terminal would have been, roughly. But there's no door, just cinder blocks, so they aren't sure of its purpose. As far as they know, there's nothing where the other end is. Just the plains."

"Doomsday prepper?" Sofia guessed.

Jason shrugged. "That'd be my guess. Back when the Rocky Mountain Arsenal was active, I bet war fears were high. Kinda surprised they've never found other half-assed shelters out there in those plains." He looked around the table. "They want us to go in, figure out what's what. Ideally, without blowing anything up or causing problems for their expansion project. Per Rafferty, the ideal outcome is anything that lets them continue excavation for the cargo annex."

Scarlet, still looking at her tablet, said, "Maybe the rumors are true." Everyone turned to her. She looked up. "What? You never read about any of the rumors about Denver International Airport?" Three heads shook. She sighed. "Back in the late eighties and early nineties when they were finishing it, after many, many delays, it was rumored that the Illuminati, the X-Men, and who knows who else had built secret bases and whatnot underneath the airport. Hence the delays."

Niles raised a hand. "What's an ex-man?"

Scarlet rolled her eyes. She pointed to Jason. "Jace'll explain it. I'm going to pack. When are we leaving?"

Jason looked at his watch. "Assuming your new toy is fast, two hours?"

From across the room, near the elevator, Scarlet said, "Oh, she's fast. We're having dinner in Denver."

Sofia and Niles rose, as well, nodding their agreement. The former slowed until it was just her and Jason. "I get that they want it to be some old bomb shelter or whatever, but it could be anything. We going strapped?"

Jason sighed. "I'm hoping it's the Illuminati." He shrugged. "But, yeah."

When she got in the elevator, Scarlet changed her mind and pressed the button for the ground floor instead of the floor with everyone's rooms. On her way to her workshop, Scarlet passed the mooring where the *Raven* bobbed in her slip. She waved.

As the lights in her workshop came to life, she rolled to the wall of blinking server racks. "Okay, Oracle. We're heading to Denver, let's get you ready to go." For the test flight, Scarlet had loaded the plane's onboard systems with analysis and data acquisition software. Now she had to make room for Oracle's core systems.

"Yes, Scarlet. I have just finished a diagnostic of the rack aboard the *Peregrine*. Everything checks out. I will be fine. Cramped, but fine," the ceiling speaker replied.

Scarlet ran a hand through her bright red hair. She had dyed a black streak into it after the Canada job, and it was almost fully grown out. "Okay, start the transfer."

"Acknowledged."

Back in the main building on the fourth floor, Niles was in his room packing the bag he hadn't even finished unpacking after Arizona.

A knock at the door stopped him. "Enter."

Jason opened the door and leaned in. "How familiar with Colorado's indigenous peoples are you?"

The big man wagged his open hand. "So-so. Why? You can't possibly think it was one of the native tribes that built whatever it is under the airport." He rubbed his chin. "If I recall correctly, that area was predominately Shoshone, Ute, and Cheyenne. None of whom build underground facilities. Certainly, none with steel doors and explosive booby-traps."

Jason shrugged. "I don't, but I wanted to make sure we could intelligently rule it out. At a minimum, we may need to identify artifacts. Thanks." He vanished back out into the hall, closing the door behind him.

Niles looked at his bag and then made a slow turn to take in his room. The living spaces that Jason built into the Expedition, Inc. building were larger than any place he had ever lived. Were they worth being shot at sometimes? He shrugged and pulled a blazer from his closet. He held it up and put it back in the closet. He grabbed another and folded it into his bag.

Jason's head appeared in Scarlet's open door. "All good with your new toy? I don't want to die over the Rocky Mountains. I've seen that movie too many times." He winked.

She rotated her chair. "I mean, you wouldn't have to suffer long; we'd eat you first." She chomped her teeth, making a clicking noise. "But yeah, we're good. I just got back from my lab. Oracle is copying her core functions into the servers aboard the plane. I had to offload the test suites I installed. She'll be fine. We'll be fine."

"You gonna be okay with Rufus and your drones?"

She shrugged. "I don't have much of a choice—can't sail the *Raven* to Denver. The *Peregrine* isn't without toys, though." She grinned.

Jason smiled, leaning away from the door.

After laughing, Scarlet said, "Oracle should be running a final set of diagnostics in the next twenty minutes or so."

Jason nodded. "Cool. So, I'm leaning toward one of your theories."

The hacker raised both hands. "Not *my* theories. I just read them aloud."

"You believe 'em?"

She shrugged. "I dunno. If you had asked me last year, I'd have said no. Then we found a secret Japanese World War Two bio-weapons lab hidden on—in—an island off the coast of Canada, so..." She shrugged again. "I can't say I don't believe that something is out there." She grinned. "I mean, you've been to Denver. Even after two expansions, that airport is still in the middle of the prairie, with nothing around for miles. Be a good place for a secret bunker or superhero base." She snapped her fingers. "Maybe it's a secret Mormon generation ship that they'll launch into space?"

"As long as we get licensing rights, I guess," Jason said.

"Scarlet, transfer complete," Oracle said from the ceiling. "Level one diagnostic underway."

The team genius looked up. "Awesome." She turned to Jason. "Better go pack. Our plane is almost ready."

An hour later, the entire team was standing outside the *Peregrine* on the office park helipad.

"It looks like a spaceship," Niles said, coming around the side after walking around the plane.

"That's what I said," Sofia agreed.

"It's weird looking," Niles said, tilting his head.

From inside the craft, Oracle said, "You are welcome to walk to Denver, Professor Kumalo."

Sofia and Jason both pursed their lips and turned to Niles, eyes wide.

The heavyset academic tutted. "No need to be sensitive, my dear. I love you for you, not your physical form."

"Okay, come on. Let's get this show on the road," Jason urged. He turned to Niles. "You can make up with Oracle en route."

Scarlet led the way onto the craft. Everyone tossed their bags onto one of the two stacked beds in the small bunk room on the left.

Sofia dropped into the pilot's seat, Scarlet was locked into her spot, and Jason took the third and final station. He wasn't sure what the station was supposed to do, but it had lots of displays and a full keyboard. Niles had been more than happy to drop onto the sofa with a book.

Sofia was tapping icons on the mostly-screen-based pilot console. "Pre-flight looks good, Oracle."

"Thank you, Sofia."

From her station, Scarlet said, "Batteries are fully charged. Oracle's primary systems are instantiated and running at 100 percent."

Jason looked at the two women. "My station has lots of

blinking lights." When they turned to him, he shrugged. He spotted an icon and tapped it. "Boarding ramp closed."

Scarlet sighed. Sofia chuckled.

Sofia watched a status screen as the twin CFM57 engines spun up to a dull roar outside.

Jason looked at Scarlet. "Those are...loud."

She turned and winked. "Wait until we're airborne."

As if waiting for that cue, the four VTOL ducts under the wings opened, allowing the craft to raise straight up into the air.

"We have received airspace clearance from San Diego International," Oracle said from the overhead speaker.

Sofia nodded. "You have the flight plan." On her displays, a map appeared with their planned route.

The matte black plane rose to an altitude of 100 feet. It turned east and tilted forward as the powerful electric jet engines powered up to full. The VTOL ducts under the wings first shifted to provide forward motion before closing to allow the twin CFM57 engines to take over.

"Off we go," Sofia said. As the craft rose higher and higher, it headed east over El Cajon.

PART TWO

CHAPTER 6

The *Peregrine* was somewhere over the Rockies and was bumping and tilting wildly. A storm to the north was kicking up all kinds of wind and rain.

"We should have flown commercial," Niles mumbled to himself. He was gripping the arm of the sofa nearest him. His knuckles were white. He was alone in the open lounge space behind the cockpit.

Despite the violent shaking that kept causing him to drop his drink, he had to admit that the furnishings were quite nice. Scarlet had excellent taste. The sofa was light brown leather with dark accents. The chair opposite him was upholstered in the same colors, but reversed. Niles wasn't a fan of the effect, but the overall aesthetic was nice. And it wasn't his airplane, so... As the plane shook again, he wondered who owned the plane? Jason? Scarlet?

The cockpit door slid open and Jason walked out, hands gripping both sides of the door frame. He made his way to the single chair opposite the sofa and next to a small workstation, dropping into the seat. "They kicked me out."

Niles held his drink up in toast. "What did you do?"

Jason rose and moved to the small pantry and serving area. Holding onto the bulkhead with one hand, grabbing a beer with the other, he said, "Nothing! I merely suggested that Sofia might—" The plane shook, leaving the two men's stomachs several feet above them. Jason rushed to the chair, continuing, "be better suited to getting us over the mountains."

"You mean the computer is still flying?" Niles asked, rubbing his forehead.

"The computer is, and will try to not take offense at your lack of faith," Oracle said from the speaker in the ceiling.

Jason grimaced. Niles chuckled. The plane rocked back and forth.

Niles took a sip of drink, savoring it. He looked over at Jason. "So, I'm thinking of going back to teaching, full time..." The statement hung in the air between the two men.

Jason took a sip of his beer. Lowering it, he said, "Okay. Like part time faculty, here and there? Or something more permanent?"

Niles waved a hand. "I love you all like children." Seeing Jason's expression, he said, "Like family." He smiled. "It seems that our exploits in Canada have garnered enough attention that the stain on my career appears to have faded."

Jason nodded. "That's good to hear." He took a sip.

"I didn't think it would ever happen, you understand. I thought my time in academia was over." Jason nodded. "Asako was instrumental in that, and from there, the few engagements I've booked have all been quite positive."

Jason took another sip. "So, greener pastures?" He smiled. He knew the other man was agonizing over this, that Niles thought Jason would be mad. But Jason figured something like this was coming, eventually.

"Well, no. But, well...you knew when you brought me on that research and academia were my first loves. Field work was never my thing."

The plane tilted severely enough that both men had to scramble to tilt their drinks to keep them from sloshing.

"So, now that you got what you want, you're casting us aside?" Jason said, trying his best to keep a straight face. The disappointment was real, but he couldn't be mad at his friend. Niles was right—field work had never been his thing. Jason, Sofia, even Scarlet, probably enjoyed the thrill of the chase, the occasional gunfire. Niles never did.

"Oh, dear. Jason, no, of course not," Niles stammered.

Jason held up his free hand. "Niles, I'm fucking with you. I couldn't be happier for you."

The other man stared at Jason unblinking, his mouth hanging open. When he recovered, he said, "You are a cruel person." Then he broke into a wide, toothy grin.

Jason smiled. "I won't lie. I'm sad to see you go and hope we can call on you from time to time, but I kinda knew deep down it was never permanent." He raised his bottle in toast, Niles matching the gesture from across the small space. "You pick a school?" He waved a hand before

Niles could answer. "Actually, more importantly, have you figured out how to break it to Scarlet?"

Niles' face fell. "I had hoped you'd tell her."

Jason almost did a spit take, shaking his head. "Oh no. This is all you. Good luck."

The *Peregrine* touched down in a corner of the airport set aside for private craft and VIPs. The control tower had more than a few questions for the oddly configured private plane that came in requesting a VTOL landing pad.

After clearing the rougher air over the Rockies, the rest of the flight had been smooth. Unbeknownst to Jason and Niles, Sofia and Scarlet had told Oracle to put the *Peregrine* through its paces.

Despite the months of simulations, Oracle had found that actual piloting was considerably more difficult than she had expected. The plane's unique design had created tremendous problems for the intelligence at the start, as she came to understand the craft's flight properties. Once she had that down, the flight was smooth and Oracle's computerized confidence in how the craft handled rose.

By the time they landed in Denver, she was successfully modeling out dozens of permutations for every possible maneuver the plane might need to make.

The plane eased to a stop fifty feet above its assigned landing pad and dropped to a soft touchdown.

Waiting outside the plane, Melissa Rafferty leaned

over to JK Scheinberg and Clark Haggerty. "That's different."

The barrel-chested security contractor harrumphed. "Showy nonsense."

JK looked at the odd plane, then at the intimidating mercenary, but said nothing.

Haggerty had been in a foul mood since one of his men had been killed in the explosion in the tunnel and the drones he sent in to investigate had found nothing. He had argued over and over with Melissa and the airport's chief executive to let him bring in more people. They could clear the tunnel and whatever else was beyond it if he had more manpower, he insisted.

To no avail. They had both refused, insisting that the occupants of the weird plane before him were professionals, and this was right in their wheelhouse. After some internet searching, he was even less thrilled to have strangers around than he had been before. The thing in Canada in sounded like a complete cluster fuck. How Latricia thought these idiots would somehow do a better job than his well-trained teams was beyond him.

With the hiss of escaping gas, the ramp eased to the tarmac. Inside, Jason turned to Scarlet. "What was that hissing sound?"

She grinned. "Special effects."

From the back of the foursome, Niles groaned.

Jason shushed them all. "Come on, they're waiting." He hefted his duffel bag onto his shoulder and marched down the ramp.

He met the welcoming committee, made and received

introductions, and then said, "Thanks for calling us in on this. It sounds like an exciting find."

Haggerty growled. "It's not a find. It's an impediment to the project, and a security risk."

Jason raised an eyebrow. Next to the big angry military man, the less athletic one said, "He's not wrong. The sooner we can get back to work, the better. My team's on-time bonus is already in jeopardy."

Jason nodded. "Understood, of course. We'll do our best to get this thing figured out quickly and let you know what you're dealing with."

Niles stepped forward. "You're in good hands."

Haggerty turned and headed toward the waiting van, opening the passenger door and getting in. Jason had made it clear that they'd require accessible transport while in Denver. Melissa and JK extended their hands, the former saying, "This way. We'll get you settled at the hotel." She gestured to a strange bow-tie-shaped building at the end of the terminal structure. Everyone followed her, piling into the van.

The ride back to the airport building was awkward, to say the least. Finally, Sofia decided to break the silence. She leaned forward in her seat. "So, Mr. Haggerty. What service?"

He barely turned his head. "Marines. Only way to serve."

"Hoorah," Sofia agreed.

The gray-haired man turned fully in the seat. "You served?" His eyebrow was arched as he looked her up and down. His expression said he wasn't impressed.

Jason groaned.

Sofia smiled and listed off her tours of duty. The grumpy security man listened, his frown easing into a smile until she got to her discharge.

"Guess you're not really a jarhead, then." He turned in his seat.

Jason and Scarlet's reflexes were the only things that kept Sofia from leaping into the front of the van.

Melissa, driving the van, pulled up to a stop. "Here we are."

In the very back of the van, JK turned to Latricia and whispered, "This should be interesting." She turned, glaring.

Melissa parked the van in a service alley behind the airport hotel.

From behind, the distinct shape of the hotel was hard to determine. Scarlet remembered staying there with her family on a vacation to the Rocky Mountains before she went off to college.

Melissa continued, "We'll meet you in the lobby at eight." Nods all around.

As the team walked into the hotel, Scarlet said, "I could use a nightcap."

Getting checked into the hotel was fast and easy, and the bellmen were more than happy to take their bags and deliver them to the suites that the airport arranged for the Expedition, Inc. team.

The suite was near the top of the oddly shaped bow tie building. It was actually two suites connected via French doors. Looking around, Sofia wasn't sure what type of president or rock star would normally need such a space.

In total, the suite was four bedrooms, two kitchenettes, and two lounge spaces with sofas, chairs, and big flat panel screens mounted on the walls.

Everyone took a few minutes to get themselves situated in their respective rooms before meeting at what Scarlet called Lounge One, which connected to Jason's and her rooms.

"Ready to eat?" Jason asked, receiving three vehement head nods.

After getting directions to the light rail station, the team was sitting comfortably as the still mostly empty prairie that surrounded the airport sped by in the dark.

Sofia broke the silence. "So that jarhead mercenary, Haggerty, is gonna be an issue."

Niles nodded his agreement. "He seemed especially disgruntled by our presence."

Jason shrugged. "There's always someone that feels threatened. Remember that weaselly little vice president fella at Global Acquisitions? He was so sure we'd put him out of a job." The others responded with nods and chuckles.

Sofia remained serious. "We should keep an eye on him. I have a bad feeling."

"Because you two got into it in the van?" Scarlet asked.

Sofia shook her head. "No, I had that *puta* pegged the

moment I saw the haircut. The rest just confirmed it. I told my story to get a feel for what type of man he is."

"And?" Niles prodded.

"Not a good man," Sofia said.

Jason mulled it over. "He does seem to think blowing up or paving over whatever is down there is the best policy."

The light rail car slowed, the automated announcement saying, "Union Station, downtown Denver." They all stood, along with a dozen or two other riders.

Exiting the transit station into the late evening rush of downtown Denver, Jason said, "Anyone have any recommendations?"

Downtown Denver was no Manhattan but certainly was no slouch in the glass-and-steel-tower game. Union Station sat surrounded by ten- and twenty-story buildings that stood dwarfed by the forty- and sixty-story monsters a few blocks away in the city's financial and central business districts.

Scarlet raised a hand. "Follow me. Yelp Elite for five years running. I found us a cool spot." She guided her chair down the pedestrian mall that connected the bustling transit hub to the rest of downtown. Buses, at one time, rumbled up and down the mall, stopping at every block. Some time ago, the buses were moved to the blocks on either side. That had boosted business and foot traffic on the mall several times over. The side streets connecting the bus route to the mall also saw boosts in business income.

The group walked and rolled for several blocks before Scarlet called a halt.

Niles looked around. "My dear, there's nothing here." He pointed to the nearest storefront, covered in brown paper. Across the mall was a store selling baseball caps and jerseys. Nothing else nearby seemed open, or even seemed to be a restaurant, for that matter.

Scarlet made a face that conveyed more contempt than Jason would have thought possible, causing the large South African man to take a step back.

She steered her chair around the corner into an alleyway and to a ramp that led to a door set back into the damp-looking brick. Over the door was a small metal sign, a bowl and chopsticks etched into it. She rang a doorbell that no one else had noticed.

The door opened, and as Scarlet entered, she looked over her shoulder. "Thank me later."

Inside, lit only by dim red lighting was the most exquisite ramen place Jason had ever seen. Half of the dozen or so tables were occupied, mostly couples enjoying quiet conversations amid the occasional slurp of noodles.

"Oh. Wow," Sofia whispered. Niles' head bobbed in agreement.

A young woman in a tight black velvet dress that stopped well above the knees approached. "Good evening. Reservation?"

"Kincaid," Scarlet answered.

Jason's eyebrows shot up.

"Right this way." The hostess extended an arm toward a table in the corner with enough room for Scarlet to pull up her chair.

By the time the team left the restaurant, it was nearly midnight. Niles had both hands on his belly as they exited the alley. "My goodness, that was delicious." He turned to Scarlet. "My dear, you're a miracle worker with that app thing of yours."

Scarlet smiled. "I do what I can."

The pedestrian mall was more deserted than not as they made their way back to Union Station.

Passing a woman sleeping on the steps of a bank, Niles kneeled and placed a bill under her hand. The others had slowed and turned to watch him, and as he rose, he cleared his throat.

Sofia and Jason turned as one. Three men in coats too bulky for the weather and ratty ball caps low over their faces stepped onto the sidewalk from an alley. All three looked like a good meal was a rarity.

"Nice folks like you shouldn't be out this late," the apparent spokesperson of the group said. He inclined his head to the sleeping woman. "Any more charity where that came from?"

Niles spoke up. "We're more than happy to be on our way."

"Of course," the other man said, a smile in his voice. "After you hand over your phones, wallets, and of course, purses." His eyes went to Scarlet, then Sofia.

Scarlet cocked her head. "Do either of us look like we carry purses?"

One of the men, darker-skinned than his friends, said,

"Just do it. Grab their shit, man." He was clutching a small pocketknife. He looked up and down the street.

The trio of muggers came forward. Sofia and Jason moved as one, the former going high, the latter also high. Sofia produced a wicked looking KA-BAR from her boot in a single swift motion. With a click, Jason deployed a double-edged stiletto.

Before the muggers realized the threat, the ex-Marine lunged, slashing her blade across the forearm of the man nearest her, eliciting a startled scream. She shoved Jason out of the way of a pipe arcing toward him. "You were supposed to go low."

"I thought you were," he retorted, swiping up, his blade catching the back of the black man's hand, forcing him to drop his pocket knife with a cry of pain.

Sofia ducked a sloppy kick, bobbing then weaving to the side, leaving her first opponent's reach and getting back into a fighting stance. Her first opponent did the same, sort of, now favoring his other arm.

Jason moved against the leader of the pack, coming in low this time to drive his shoulder into the man's midsection, forcing the wind out of him and sending them both tumbling to the ground. Jason was careful to not stab the man, at least at first. He planted his blade into the man's shoulder.

While Jason and Sofia were busy, the third man came at Niles and Scarlet. His hand clutched a piece of pipe similar to his friend's. "Just give us your fucking stuff, old man," the mugger said.

Scarlet rolled around Niles' side, shoving him out of the way. She was holding something out in front of her.

The man's eyes widened briefly before he squinted at the device. "What is that?"

Scarlet winked as the end of the device erupted in a bright flash of light.

Jason, Sofia, and both of their opponents turned to look at the commotion. Four mouths fell open.

"What the hell? Brian?" one of the muggers, the one cradling his wounded arm, said.

Pinned to the wall by what looked like brightly colored string cheese strands was the man who was attacking Niles and Scarlet. The pale blue filament formed a messy web nearly five feet wide, with a struggling man in the middle of it. The sticky filament pinned one of his arms to the wall, the other against his stomach. Neither could move more than an inch.

"Is that silly string?" Jason asked, head cocked.

One of the two unstuck muggers moved toward his friend. Scarlet wagged a finger. "Oh, and I called the cops." She pointed to the phone resting on the arm of her chair.

The two men looked at each other and moved to their friend, attempting to free him before the authorities arrived. They pulled and tugged at various strands, the stiff resin barely budging.

Jason motioned for everyone to form up. As a group, they made a hasty retreat up the street. In the distance, the sound of sirens was growing louder.

As the train pulled out of Union Station, Jason said, "Well, that was exciting."

"Welcome to Denver." Niles grinned.

The train ride was quiet; they had the car mostly to themselves at that hour.

A young couple in hiking clothes and big backpacks sat next to each other at the far end of the train, likely off on an outdoor adventure somewhere.

CHAPTER 7

Standing in the open French doors that connected the two suites, Jason clapped his hands. "Come on, come on. We're gonna be late."

He and Sofia were dressed and waiting. Niles hopped out of his room, trying to slip a dress shoe on. "Sorry, sorry. The outlet I plugged my phone into to charge, apparently was tied to the light switch." He held up his phone as evidence.

Scarlet rolled out of her room. Jason turned. "Plug your phone into the wrong socket?"

She shook her head. "Nope, just overslept." She grinned. Jason groaned.

Sofia held open the door. "*Vamos.*"

"Good morning," Melissa Rafferty said as the Expedition, Inc. team crossed the elaborate walkway connecting the hotel to the airport terminal building. She offered her hand to each of them.

Jason smiled. "Ready to show us the great mystery?"

The project manager nodded and held her hand out toward the terminal. "Sooner the better. Let's go."

Scarlet rolled up next to Melissa. "So, this tunnel. You're sure it's not part of a secret X-Men base? Or the Illuminati bunker?" She smirked. "Don't want to piss them off."

The other woman paused, turning to look down. "Um, I don't know what that means?"

Sofia chuckled from behind the pair.

From around a corner ahead, someone spoke. "It's a chocolate factory. Run by the Illuminati," said a middle-aged man with more hair on his face than his head.

Scarlet laughed. "I like you." JK Scheinberg laughed.

The team followed the airport people through tunnels, down staircases, and then through more service tunnels. As the airport expanded over the years, the underground city that made it work did, too, often not nearly as cleanly and tidily as the upstairs areas.

JK handed everyone a hard hat. Melissa Rafferty said, "I'll leave you with JK." She looked at the pudgy construction manager. "Holler if you need me." He nodded. She nodded to the Expedition, Inc. team and departed.

As the group entered the first phase cavern, Jason said, "So, how's the project going? I mean overall."

JK shrugged. "As you'd expect any public, privately funded construction project to be going. We're behind schedule, over budget, and under the gun. The governor wants it done before the next election, ideally early enough that she can campaign on it. The CEO—you met her—

wants it done yesterday." He rolled his free hand. "Same old, same old."

Niles nodded. "And now you're stuck until we finish our exploration and examination?"

All around them, men and women were working on setting up rebar forms to create walls, floors, and ceilings. Electricians and other tradespeople were laying equipment and prepping the Phase 1 site for whatever was next.

Stepping over a gridwork of iron, JK said, "Sorta. I put the crew to work here. We weren't technically going to do walls, floors, and such yet, but better than paying them to sit around, or not paying them and losing them." He pointed generally back the way they came. "That'll only last a few weeks, at best."

They reached the Phase 2 area of the dig site. Equipment and vehicles were parked where they were a few days before, when the tunnel was found. Jason and Sofia approached the tunnel opening, looking at the busted cinder blocks, powerful flashlight beams playing up and down both directions of the tunnel.

Jason pointed in the western direction. "And this way is just the wall?"

JK nodded. "Yup. Goes a hundred or two feet, then dead ends. From the images we got from Clark's folks, looks like whoever built the thing just stopped. As far as we can tell, it was probably supposed to end, connecting to the terminal. Something caused the original building plans to shift, and the tunnel was never connected." He shrugged.

Another voice, deeper, and unfortunately familiar,

said, "My people confirmed that there's no connection or even prep work for a connection over there. Dead end."

Everyone turned.

"You all met Clark Haggerty," JK said. His enthusiasm, or lack thereof, was obvious.

The burly security head joined the group, followed by two of his black-clad goons for hire. "I'll be sending some of my people in with you."

Jason held up a hand. "I don't think that's a—"

"Not open for discussion," the other man interrupted. "It's bad enough you're here. I can't have you roaming around on your own. The security of the airport, and the city and county of Denver's investments, all rests on my shoulders."

"Afraid we'll steal something?" Niles asked mildly, putting a calming hand on Sofia's forearm.

Jason sighed. "So long as it's clear, this is our operation. Your folks are welcome to join us from behind. Where they will stay." When the other man opened his mouth, Jason held up a hand. "Not negotiable. If we walk, and we will, you'll be stuck for who knows how long trying to clear all this up, further delaying your precious project." Haggerty nodded. "Good."

Jason and Sofia turned east. Jason stopped. "Uh, why is there a skull in here?"

"*Mierda*," Sofia whispered.

JK shrugged, and Niles craned his neck to look. The latter turned to Jason and Sofia. "That's disturbing."

"I wanna see," Scarlet complained. At the end of each armrest was a touch screen control panel. She tapped a few commands into the panel on the left armrest.

Niles, JK, and Clark all turned to look at a growing noise coming from Scarlet's chair. The two larger wheels looked as if they were deflating; ridges appeared as the inner frame became exposed, creating knobs and grooves.

The two smaller directional wheels did the same, a metal frame extending from the sides to move the wheels into a wider off-road-friendly configuration.

"Uh, wow," JK Scheinberg said, wide-eyed.

"You're mighty handy," the gruff mercenary commander said.

Scarlet winked and guided the chair over the lip of rubble at the tunnel opening. "Ew, gross. It is a skull." A pair of headlights flipped on from either side of her chair.

Jason turned. "Did you think we were making it up?"

Scarlet shrugged.

Niles kneeled down to get a closer look at the skull, fully illuminated by Scarlet's headlights. He gingerly poked it, then looked up. "It is fake."

"What?" most of the group said at once.

He picked the skull up. "Plastic." He looked at JK and Clark. "Did no one even look at it closely?"

"Why the hell would we get close to a human skull?" JK retorted. "That's gross. No thanks."

Niles sighed, tossing the Halloween decoration to the

ground. "Someone involved in whatever this was, had a sense of humor."

Clark Haggerty cleared his throat. "If you're all done screwing around..." He motioned to two of his people, who had joined the team in the tunnel. To them, he said, "Keep in touch."

"Yes, sir," the pair said in unison.

Jason motioned for Sofia to lead the way. "Don't forget—there's at least one unexploded booby trap."

She nodded.

Scarlet and Niles brought up the rear with the two security men. The former looked up. "So, mercenaries, huh?"

The taller of the two, a blond-haired man in his mid-forties who looked like the gym was his second home—but without looking like he was the Incredible Hulk's stunt double—said, "We don't like to use that word." He looked down. "But, yeah."

The other—a younger, leaner redhead—scolded, "Chief said to keep it professional." He met Scarlet's gaze and glared.

The blond man frowned and turned his attention forward as the group moved further into the tunnel.

Their first stop in the tunnel was the section that was strewn with debris and had nearly collapsed. SPS had already retrieved the body of their fallen colleague, and JK's team had come in to clear as much of the debris as they could to make the tunnel more passable. It was a lucky break that Scarlet's now off-road capable wheelchair was able to fit through the narrow pass that had been cleared.

They reached the second tripwire that the SPS forces had found. Jason produced a glow stick, breaking it and dropping it before the line. He placed another on the other side of the nearly invisible filament, then stepped over it.

He kneeled next to the wall where the thin line vanished into a hole drilled in the cinderblock. "This is kinda freaky. I mean, this is next level."

On the other side of the line, Sofia kneeled down. "They really put some thought into this. There's literally no easy way to disarm it."

Jason nodded.

The wiry SPS officer coughed. Scarlet looked up and sighed. In her head, she had already labeled him Grumpy Cat.

Sofia frowned and stepped over the line, holding her light on it so Niles could follow. She looked at Scarlet. Eyebrows raised, she said, "Uh, *chica?*" Her eyes met Scarlet's, then moved to the tripwire.

The crimson-haired computer hacker grinned. "Oh, no. I'm not getting left behind this time." She tapped a control on the arm of her chair.

Four distinct clunks came from beneath Scarlet's chair, followed by four thin pieces of metal sliding out from underneath, two in the front and two in the rear.

The two security men stepped away from the once again transforming chair. Niles looked at Jason, who shrugged.

"How many modes that thing have?" the blond-haired man asked no one in particular. Niles shrugged.

After a minute, the noises stopped and Scarlet looked around. "Well?" When everyone looked at her expectantly, she said, "My chair isn't going to carry itself over that tripwire."

Jason tilted his head. "What?"

"Those aren't like spider legs or something?" Grumpy Cat asked. The blond—Scarlet dubbed him Thor—leaned over a bit to look at the chair's underside.

Scarlet sighed. "No, dummies. They're handles." She pointed to Grumpy Cat, then Thor next to her. "You two, pick me up, carry me over the tripwire." She smiled. "Cleopatra style."

Both SPS men stared at her a moment. Thor wasn't as quick as his smaller colleague, who realized that the four metal extrusions were simple handles.

The two men deposited the chair safely on the other side of the booby trap. With a tap of the same icon on her control panel, the metal handles retracted back into the bottom of Scarlet's chair. She looked at the others. "You thought this thing just changed into whatever I need it to?" Nods all around. She sighed.

In the small plane hangar about as far from the dig site as possible, the *Peregrine* was sitting all alone.

Once the team had deplaned, an airport crew had come and guided the odd-looking plane into a long-term service hangar. Scarlet had warned the AI that such a thing would happen, so the plane hadn't resisted.

Since then, the AI had spent her time probing the airport's wireless networks and watching what little of the world she could see through the half open hangar doors. Thankfully, Scarlet had embedded several cameras in the sleek craft's hull.

Several hours earlier, the sleek Gulfstream that had been parked nearby had taxied out, leaving the matte black craft all alone. It had taken less than fifteen minutes to trace the plane's tail number through five different shell corporations until finally identifying the owner as a wealthy business executive with ties to two different Russian oligarchs. To kill a few additional minutes, Oracle had accessed a server in the local Internal Revenue Service office, flagging the craft. She could not tell if the men who came to lead the plane out of the hangar were with the government or not.

Since then, it had been just the *Peregrine* alone in the hangar, until a pair of airport employees in reflective vests entered. Oracle watched the pair via the *Peregrine*'s cameras. They looked at the tool chests near where the other plane had been parked.

Finally, the two men took notice of the unusual plane and moved in closer. The taller of the two ran his hand along the fuselage. "Damn, this thing is sick."

"Right?" his friend agreed. "Think it's open?"

"One way to find out," the other replied. He made a slow circle around the *Peregrine*. "There's no fucking doors," he declared.

"Shut up, dummy. There have to be doors." Both men were dark-skinned, wearing vests and hard hats. Thick over-the-ear headsets hung on both of their necks.

The slightly taller of the two took his hat off, revealing a shiny hairless head. "Maybe there's a ramp? This thing sits low enough." He moved to the rear of the plane. "You dumb ass." He jabbed a finger at the raised ramp.

"Is it military?" the shorter one asked.

"Doesn't look it," the taller one replied, running his fingers along the seam of the ramp, trying to find a release. He turned to his friend. "There's a crowbar in that tool chest with the stickers on it."

From the small camera tucked under the plane's tail, above the ramp, Oracle watched this exchange. She knew that Scarlet and the others were already beyond comm range, underground.

After computing several thousand courses of action, Oracle made a decision. The twin electric engines on the ends of the stubby wings clicked twice, then spun up.

"Holy shit!" the short interloper shouted, dropping the crow bar to the ground.

Jason had convinced Scarlet to retire the drone *Emmet* from use aboard the *Raven*, but not from service in general. A hatch on the top of the plane slid open revealing the aged, but dependable, drone.

The *Peregrine* rotated on her stubby wheeled landing gear. Because the gears were so short, Scarlet had engineered them to allow the plane to spin a full 360 degrees in place.

Wishing she had access to external speakers, Oracle

instead activated every external light she could in as jarring a pattern as possible.

The taller man ducked as the wing-mounted engine slid toward him. He hit the ground and scrambled toward his friend.

While the intruders were busy, *Emmet* the drone launched. From her new vantage point, Oracle saw her two harassers. *Emmet* dove at the first, banking to charge the other.

The two screamed as they ran for the door, *Emmet* hot on their heels. Careful to not hurt them, she drove *Emmet* into the back of the nearest man, pushing him to the ground.

"Get away from us!" the smaller one screamed. He lashed out with a sloppy kick at the hovering *Emmet*. The drone did not even have to dodge, the kick went so wide. The first man scrambled to his feet, pushing his friend through the door.

Emmet rose and returned to its docking port on the back of the *Peregrine*.

Niles leaned back from the heavy steel door. "Fifty years, tops." He smiled at Sofia as he dusted his hands on his cargo pants. "Not Japanese." After the tripwire, it had been an uneventful march to the locked steel door that SPS's drone found earlier. The tunnel was relatively clean, showing little to no wear and tear. That it was constructed with cinderblocks was still a mystery, but Jason and the others liked those.

Sofia grinned.

The smaller security man—Matt, they had learned—looked at his colleague, Bryan, and said, "Japanese?" Bryan shrugged. Neither were familiar with Expedition, Inc.'s past exploits.

Scarlet looked at the two black-clad men. She still preferred Grumpy Cat and Thor.

Jason reached past Niles to try the handle. The door didn't budge. At all. He looked over his shoulder at everyone staring at him. "Worth a shot."

Matt and Bryan looked at each other again.

Jason reached into a thigh pocket in his cargo pants, withdrawing a small plastic clamshell case. Snapping it open, he produced a small glass vial and sprinkled the clear liquid on the two heavy iron hinges and, using an eyedropper that was in the same case, injected the liquid into the lock's keyhole.

Everyone stepped back as thin wisps of acrid smoke wafted from the hinges and lock.

Bryan, the SPS man, started, "Is it supposed—" With a groan of tortured metal, the door sagged and thudded to the floor before pitching forward. "That?"

Nodding, Jason said, "More or less." He stepped over the door and through the threshold.

Scarlet sighed and pressed the control to activate what she now called "Cleopatra mode." She motioned to Bryan and Matt, the former grumbling as he kneeled to lift her chair through the threshold. She had to admit, she was tempted to make them carry her the entire time.

The chamber on the other side of the door wasn't like anything any of them were expecting. It was a wide circular space with mid-century chairs and sofas scattered around coffee tables and potted, obviously fake, plants.

From behind one of the sofas, a multi-limbed matte black light fixture reached up and over, each limb ending in a bulb-shaped light housing.

A fine blanket of dust covered every horizontal surface, including a few scattered magazines and books.

Niles moved his flashlight beam around the room. "My goodness." He was beside himself. The Japanese island was the find of a lifetime, and here he was, discovering this —whatever it was.

Jason released a low whistle. When Niles met his gaze, the younger man winked. Niles frowned.

"*Mierda*, this is weird," Sofia said to no one in particular. Niles' flashlight beam fell across a potted palm that was leaning, tipped over against the opposite wall.

Scarlet's headlights crossed a vending machine as she made a slow circle. "Holy, shit. Is that a BarNone?" She rolled toward the ancient machine.

The two security men fanned out from the doorway, making a slow circuit around the room's perimeter. Almost opposite the door they came in through was an arched doorway that led to a downward spiraling ramp. Matt looked at his colleague. "At least we don't have to carry that crippled girl."

Bryan punched the younger man in the shoulder.

"One, she's hot. Two, and most important, don't be so fucking gross." He shook his head.

"What?" the smaller man replied. He flinched when his colleague turned, glaring, fist held at the ready.

Jason took in the room. "Okay, this is cool, but what the hell is this?" He played his flashlight beam around the room one more time, taking in the oddly old—but in excellent shape—decor.

Scarlet chimed in, "Well, it ain't the X-Men, that's for sure."

Sofia rolled her eyes.

Niles said, "This is intriguing. This room, I presume the entire facility, was built in the 1980s or '90s." His flashlight illuminated the coffee table and its assortment of dust covered magazines.

"Like, totally," Scarlet said under her breath as she rolled around one of the chairs. She pointed to the doorway the two security men were standing near. "Let's see how deep the rabbit hole goes."

"I'm a bit surprised this facility is so accessible," Niles said to Sofia as they fell in behind Scarlet and Jason.

Jason reached the archway and looked down. "Pretty steep." He reached into a satchel at his hip, removing a small half circle the size of a softball. He toggled a small switch then slapped the device against the wall. A second passed, then the half orb blazed to life, illuminating a good portion of the room.

He smiled. "Stick-ems."

Scarlet pinched him, sending him out of her way. She

rolled easily down the concrete ramp. "Thank you, old-timey contractors following ADA guidelines."

Everyone followed.

The ramp wound round and round for what, to Jason, felt like forever. His flashlight beam finally hit another open arched doorway. The light from Scarlet's headlights was already dim.

The room was circular, like the one above it. Where the one above was some type of sitting room or foyer, this one was clearly meant to be a research lab. Researching what, wasn't clear. Polished metal tables filled the space, all of them empty. Along the curved walls, several empty shelving units stood silent vigil. Whatever was supposed to happen in this room never did.

"What the..." Jason said, playing his flashlight beam along the wall. "There's nothing here."

Matt, the smaller security man, clapped his hands. "Welp, guess that's that. You can get your check and get the hell out of here."

Jason turned toward him. "Not until we've explored the entire facility, or whatever this is."

The smaller man squared off in front of Jason. "It's an empty bunker. Probably some prepper nut from the '80s or something. That's it, end of story."

Jason shook his head. "And we'll know exactly what, when we're finished." He turned, producing a stick-em, slapping it against the wall.

As the room brightened, the other man growled. "I say we get back topside, blow that tunnel, and let the dirt movers get back to work."

Sofia clucked, but otherwise kept her opinion to herself.

Jason smiled. "Well, you're welcome to do what you like. We were hired to check this place out and report back. We didn't ask for your company, and we're not being paid by your paramilitary boy scout leader. We're going to do the job we're being paid to do, and you and your crew-cut-wearing boss can suck it." He turned but stopped short when the security man gripped his shoulder.

Sofia took a step closer. "Think this through," she ground out.

The bigger security agent said, "Dude. Cool it." He put his hand on his colleague's shoulder.

Jason met Matt's eyes. "I'd listen to them."

"Or what?"

Jason's gaze flicked to Sofia. "Or she pulls your arms out of their sockets and beats you to death with them." He tilted his head. "While I watch, giggling."

Niles, standing a dozen or more meters away near the opposite wall, said, "Jason, look at this." He had been doing his best to ignore the testosterone fest taking place by the doorway.

He was standing next to some type of structural support member. Similar structures lined the circular space every few meters, rising to the ceiling, then forming a spoke-like structure connecting in the center of the ceiling where a large circular light fixture hung. The room above had been of a similar spoke and wheel design.

Jason looked at his opponent one last time, then turned and walked over to join Niles. He put a hand on the support. It was cold to the touch, rough. "Concrete." He looked around. "Incredible engineering."

Niles nodded. "Seems almost new. No cracks or deterioration." He ran a hand along the support column.

The tall SPS officer, Bryan, said, "Looks like there are two ways out of this one." He pointed his flashlight beam at an arched doorway like the one they had come in through, then to another a few yards along the wall. Through the first was another spiraling ramp heading further down. Through the other, a staircase up.

"Guess we know which way I'm going," Scarlet quipped. She rolled toward the doorway and ramp beyond.

"Jace?" Sofia said.

Jason maneuvered his flashlight beam around, settling it on the pair of security men. The stick-ems did a great job of brightening the room, but the flashlight beam helped make his point. "We should split up. The sooner we clear this place, the sooner we can decide what's next. One of you with one group, one with the other?"

Matt, the smaller of the pair, scowled but nodded. "Makes sense. The chief wants this cleared up ASAP." He looked at his big friend. "I'll take the stairs."

Jason nodded. "I'll go with Scarlet and Bryan. Sofia and Niles, you're with Matt."

Sofia grinned and looked at Matt. "This will be fun."

Matt didn't wait for Sofia or Niles. He stormed through the arched opening and up the stairs.

Jason turned to Bryan. "Your friend is a peach." He

headed after Scarlet, the big SPS man falling in behind him.

The staircase went up a short way before opening into a room almost as big as the one they just left. This room was rectangular and filled with floor-to-ceiling shelves, several rows of them. Unlike the research room and its empty stainless steel, these shelves were dingy and full.

Matt was already moving down one row. Boxes of all shapes and sizes filled nearly all the shelf space.

Sofia reached the nearest shelf and took a box down. She reached inside and removed a can. "Canned peaches."

"Yum," Niles offered from the next row over.

"Hey, you two! Get over here!" Matt shouted from deeper in the storeroom.

Sofia rolled her eyes, mumbling something in Spanish.

CHAPTER 8

"Hey, slow down," Jason admonished.

Scarlet was out of sight around the next bend in the sloping ramp.

"Your people seem well disciplined," Bryan said from over Jason's shoulder. "Professional, even."

He looked up and over, shrugging. "Sofia is the only one that served." He nodded to the wheelchair ahead of them. "The rest are, at best, a bag of cats."

As a kid, Jason had thought about enlisting in the military. His mom served, Army. He remembered all the moving they did, her various assignments taking them all around the country. They weren't what he'd call fond memories.

It had taken a toll on the family. His dad eventually filed for a divorce. Jason, seeking stability, had stayed with his dad, letting mom follow her career. He was entering high school and the idea of relocating as a sophomore or junior had felt like the worst possible thing in all the universe.

His dad was an engineer at a commercial shipyard in Oceanside, building luxury yachts for California's wealthiest, as well as the occasional floating corporate office park. The time with his dad, on the water, seeing so many ships, had ensured he'd never stray too far from San Diego.

He spent summers with his mom wherever she was. It had worked well enough, and being the kid who saw the world over the summer had been fun.

Despite all that, the whole thing had soured his view of being in the military.

Jason blinked, shaking the memories away. "Army?"

Bryan smiled. "How'd you know?"

Jason turned back to the arched doorway at the bottom of the ramp. "Hunch."

By the time Jason and Bryan caught up to her, Scarlet was in the middle of a square room.

"What's this?" Bryan asked, his flashlight beam playing around the room. It was empty except for a lone couch against one wall and a small table in the middle of the room. The cinder block walls looked as new as the rest of the spaces they had seen.

"Waiting room," Scarlet said from next to the table. She reached down and picked something up. She held it up for Jason's flashlight beam. A copy of *PEOPLE* magazine dated April 1993. As she moved it, a blanket of dust slid off.

Jason slapped a stick-em to the wall near the archway they just came through.

Bryan came closer to Scarlet and the table. "Damn." He looked at Scarlet. "Who's Brandon Lee?" The hacker shrugged, dropping the magazine back onto the coffee table.

Jason sighed, shaking his head. "Curiouser and curiouser," he whispered to himself. The room had a single doorway opposite the one the three of them came through. It didn't look like there was a ramp. Maybe another room?

Scarlet rolled around the table, taking in the other magazines scattered across its surface. She still couldn't piece together the purpose of the space. For an Illuminati stronghold, it didn't feel very Illuminati. For a secret super-hero base, it definitely didn't feel super. More like half complete. It seemed like a lot of effort and expense to build the world's deepest dentist office.

"Onward," Jason said, motioning forward to the archway and whatever was beyond it.

"Okay, this is something," Scarlet said as her chair's headlights splashed across racks of what looked like old school ammo cases. Racks that looked like they should have machine guns clipped into them lined the walls. Filling the middle were an assortment of shelves and work benches.

"Some type of armory?" Bryan asked, his own flashlight beam moving along the walls.

"What gave it away?" Scarlet quipped.

Jason cut off the big security man's retort. "The question is—or questions are—where are the weapons that should be here and who put them here?" He slapped a stick-em to the wall to punctuate his question.

Scarlet pulled an ammo box off the shelf nearest her.

Holding it up, she said, "I've got the answer to part two." On the side of the box, in chipped white paint, was the logo of the US Army.

Bryan came over, taking the tin from Scarlet. He shook it. "It's full."

Jason joined them. "Ammo, but no guns."

"Secret Army base?" Scarlet asked.

"To what end?" Jason replied. Scarlet and Bryan shrugged.

The big security man unclipped the radio from his belt. "I better report in."

Jason and Scarlet watched him play with the radio. The latter finally asked, "Problem?"

Bryan held the radio out. "Not getting anything."

Jason frowned, taking the device and examining the LED screen. The display showed a distinct lack of signal. He looked around. "Guess they, whomever that is, built this place to block signals." He handed the useless radio back to its owner. He nodded back the way they came. He put a hand against the wall. "Bet there's rebar all through these walls." He shrugged. "Let's head back to the first room. There was another ramp heading down."

"Someone was ready for the end of the world," Sofia said, putting down another can of preserved food, this time cocktail wieners.

The entire room was full, shelf after shelf of consumables, floor to ceiling.

"This room could feed a few dozen people for a while," Niles added. He looked around. The careful organization of supplies was incredible.

"No, thanks," Matt said from deeper in the room.

The two Expedition, Inc. team members finally joined the other man, relishing the expression on his face at how long they took to get there. He was next to a door.

"Congrats, you found a door," Sofia said.

"Fuck off," the rangy security man said. He pointed. "Open it up."

"I look like a skeleton key?" Sofia retorted, arms crossed over her chest.

"Children, please," Niles chastised as he pushed between them to examine the door. It was similar to the one they had come through to enter the facility from the tunnel. "Back door?" he wondered aloud. He reached for the handle, pushing. The door didn't budge.

Looking at the security man, he said, "You could've told me." The other man shrugged.

Sofia produced a small padded case, similar to what Jason had used earlier. The specially formulated acid made quick work of the locking mechanism. Unlike Jason, Sofia didn't apply it to the hinges. The door swung open with the screech of tortured metal.

The trio entered the next room, their flashlights roaming the walls. It was a storage room like the one they just left. Same type of shelves: freestanding and lining the walls. Niles moved to the side and removed a stick-em, affixing it to the wall. Before the device lit up, it clattered to the floor.

Sofia and Matt turned. Niles flushed. "Sorry." He fumbled for the lighting unit, sticking it to the wall. A moment later, the room was bathed in light.

Unlike the other room, this room wasn't full of consumables.

"Is that an—" Niles started.

"Igloo cooler? Yes," Sofia interrupted.

"The hell is this?" Matt said as he moved deeper into the building.

"Do you hear that?" Sofia said, stopping everyone in their tracks. She cocked her head, moving in a slow circle. "Is that an engine?" She shook her head. "Generator."

Matt moved further into the room, into the shadows at the far end.

"Is that a good idea?" Niles wondered, clicking his flashlight back on, the beam falling on the other man's back. This room was nearly twice as big as the first storage room.

Sofia moved to the shelf with the cooler on it. "These are all air cargo." She tapped her finger against a label that showed MEX -> DEN on it.

Niles rubbed his chin, looking at another package. "This one looks like it started in Luxembourg. Destination, Denver."

"They're all coming here," Sofia mumbled, running a finger along the shelf as she read labels.

"Hey!" the annoying little security man shouted.

Sofia scowled. "Man, you better stop shouting for us like we work for you." No reply. She looked over her shoulder. Niles wasn't in the same row, but she could see his flashlight beam the next row over, heading in the summons' direction. It wasn't lost on her that the mysterious noise was also in that direction.

Without warning, the lights in the room snapped on. Sofia swore. She heard Niles swear in Afrikaans.

"What the hell?" she said. "You do that?"

"Yeah, get over here and check it out," Matt replied.

Niles and Sofia exchanged a look between two aisles and headed for the third member of their team. Sofia looked at the northern wall of the room, spotting another door, similar to the one they just came in through. Another storeroom, she assumed. She and Niles reached the irritating third member of the group at the same time. He was standing next to a hole in the wall, covered with a sloppily installed security door like you'd find in a home improvement store.

The rumble of a small engine was clearer here. It was on the other side of the door. Through a small gap in the cinder blocks and the security door, a thick electric cord came into the storeroom and had been spliced into the room's existing wiring. Someone wired a light switch into the setup where the two sets of wires met.

Matt tried the handle on the door. "Locked."

Niles looked around. "Obviously, someone is using this storeroom."

"Who?" Matt said. He unclipped his radio. "Boss, we have a situation." The radio squawked. Whatever answer came back was garbled. He held the device in front of him, examining the small display. He tried again. "Chief, this is Matt. Come in."

Something, then static, then, "Repeat."

Matt explained the situation as he understood it, unsure how much of his report was making it through.

Niles looked at Sofia, worry on his face. Sofia's expression mirrored his.

Back in the main excavation site, JK Scheinberg watched Clark Haggerty make a slow circle as he filled the space with expletives. The radio in his hand was belching out more static than words. JK wasn't sure which of Haggerty's goons was trying to report in. He wasn't sure Haggerty could even tell with all the static.

Haggerty turned to a group of six of his men. "Full battle rattle. Get down there." He pointed toward the Phase 2 cavern and open cinderblock tunnel.

"Clark, Melissa was pretty clear ab—" JK started.

The big man spun on the heavyset construction manager. "Shut the fuck up." He jabbed a finger into the cavern. "Something is there. My job is to secure this airport and ensure it continues to generate a profit for the business backers."

JK frowned. He reached for his mobile phone only to have Clark slap the device out of his hands. "The fuck, man!?" His phone was lying in the dirt, now with a cracked screen.

Clark met his eyes, forcing the smaller man to blink and avert his gaze. JK took an involuntary step back.

Clark's face was a deep crimson. He hated not

knowing what was going on in that tunnel. Not being fully in control of a situation did not sit well with him, and as the hours ticked by, what passed for calm had eroded considerably.

JK picked up his phone and made a hasty retreat. He snapped his fingers at one of his people who was trying to not stare at the confrontation that just took place. "Gimme your phone!" He snapped his fingers again.

Barely ten minutes later, the six men and women strode through Cavern 1 into Cavern 2. All of them were in body armor and armed with rifles. Haggerty nodded. "Find Matt and Bryan. Bring those fucking consultants out. Nothing else matters down there."

The six armed SPS troops strutted off into Cavern 2 and the hole in the wall that led to... whatever it was down below.

JK ran a hand through what was left of his hair. This was not good. Clark seemed unhinged.

In the tunnel, the six ex-military people were moving toward the now open door.

Clark had his tablet clutched in one hand. Six small video feeds were visible, just like the last team that went into the tunnel.

No one would ever know exactly what happened, but the squad leader of the retrieval team failed to notice the faded glow sticks Jason had left behind.

All six video feeds on Clark's tablet went to static one second before the explosion rocked the cavern.

JK and the remaining construction and SPS forces scrambled as chunks of rock fell from the ceiling in both caverns. Several people screamed as chunks of dirt crashed down on them. A large crack shot through the west wall of Cavern 1.

Out in the open space several kilometers to the east of Denver International Airport, a lone radio transmission tower and its squat concrete control room stood watch over what looked, for all intents and purposes, like a whole lot of empty prairie. Inside the concrete building next to the tower, several servers blinked. Sensors on a door almost a kilometer away had just tripped. At the top of the fake radio tower, a small satellite transceiver came to life, calling home.

The ground shook, spilling dust from seams in the cinder block ceiling. Niles and Sofia glared at Matt. The security man looked at both of them. Dull fury and terror warred across his face. "The fuck did you do?" he barked, hand dropping to his hip, and the pistol holstered there.

Sofia held both hands up, palms out. "Woah there. This wasn't us." She looked from the antsy SPS officer to Niles and back. "We've been right here with you, *amigo*."

Niles nodded, looking at the door to the other storage room. A cloud of dust was working its way into the room. "If I had to guess, your people neglected to remember the trip wire in the tunnel." Just when he was beginning to get excited about this find, he was reminded of the mortal danger that came with it. Maybe his decision was right. The university was no underground bunker, but also, the only real danger was taco night.

Matt growled and pushed past the pair, and stormed back into the first storage room, causing the dust cloud to swirl around him. He flapped his hands ineffectively, trying to clear the air. The dust was so thick, the light from the stick-em in the room hardly had an impact.

Niles shook his head. "It's always the military types." He glanced at Sofia. "No offense."

She shrugged. "None taken. You're not wrong." She inclined her head. "We should follow him, make sure he does nothing to get us killed."

They headed out into the first storage room. The others would be looking to reconnect after that explosion.

They ran into Jason, Scarlet, and the big blond security man a few minutes later at the ramp that led down into the facility.

Deeper down inside the complex, Jason, Scarlet, and Bryan looked up as the room that connected to the armory shook and dust rained down on the three of them.

All three covered their heads and crouched down. If the ceiling collapsed, there'd be nothing they could do about it, but squatting felt like a safe thing to do.

"That's not good," Scarlet said, waving a hand in front of her face, trying to clear the dust. It was not working.

Bryan looked at Scarlet. "You okay?" He made a show of checking her chair over, then moving to her. She waved him off.

Jason, shielding his eyes, said, "I'm okay, thanks."

The big man shrugged. Jason sighed. "Scratch going down. We need to check on the others, and without radios, we'll have to go find them."

Scarlet and Bryan nodded.

Jason walked to the ramp they had come down and headed up. Bryan followed Scarlet as she rolled behind Jason. "So, you're the like the team genius or something?"

She was glad that the giant blond-haired security man was behind her. He didn't see her blush. The group rounded the ramp, coming into range of one of Jason's sticky light devices. She nodded. "Uh, yeah, something like that."

"Cool."

Up ahead, Jason rolled his eyes. He was thrilled that Scarlet was interested in someone, even if it was an employee of that asshole back at the dig site. He couldn't recall the last time Scarlet had had shown an interest in someone other than Oracle, let alone gone on a date.

Scarlet said, "Yeah, I'm kinda the Gadget Hackwrench of the team."

Bryan slowed, rubbing his stubble covered chin. "Oh, man. The blimp plane. I wanted one of those so bad."

Scarlet slowed to a stop, turning to look over her shoulder. "What?"

Bryan nodded. "Yeah, that thing was so awesome."

"Right?" Scarlet's head bobbed. "Gadget could build anything!"

Bryan blushed a little. "She was my favorite."

Scarlet met his blush. "Same."

From almost out of sight around the bend in the ramp, Jason sighed loud enough for Scarlet and Bryan to hear, sending a blush back up their cheeks. She said, "Uh... Anyway." She turned her chair and continued up the ramp.

Bryan smiled. "Brains are sexy," he said under his breath.

Jason's group found Niles and Sofia in the unfinished research area. "Where's the scrawny one? He blow up?"

"If only," Sofia said. She pointed to the doorway to the tunnel. "He went that way."

Bryan looked at the team, then said, "I'll go check on him."

Niles held up a hand. "It could be dangerous. Our assumption is that when Matt called your boss for reinforcements, they forgot about the trip wire."

Jason swore under his breath.

"Reinforcements?" Bryan looked at the doorway to the storage areas. He pushed the South African man aside.

Moments before Bryan reached the arched entry into the tunnel that led back to the airport, a loud rumble filled the space and shook the room. A billowing cloud of dust preceded several loud cracks and the sound of tumbling rocks. The nearest wall trembled as a fissure shot through it.

Bryan dove back into the room that they all agreed was

some type of foyer, seconds before the dust cloud filled the room.

The dust was so thick that it nearly overwhelmed the portable light fixtures, casting the room into murky half-light.

Much coughing and gagging later, Jason said, "Okay, so...Now we're trapped in here."

"Actually." Niles held up a hand.

Before he could finish his correction, the sound of a metal security door swinging open echoed down the short staircase from the storage areas.

"*Dios mio,*" Sofia whispered.

Matt Jacoby rushed through the first storeroom toward the tunnel. The dust was so thick, breathing was getting difficult. He had to pull his shirt up over his nose and mouth.

He stumbled through the empty-shelved research room. By the time he was nearing the ramp that led up to the foyer, the dust was settling, a little. He could see one of that smug dickhead Kincaid's little light fixtures. He could hear the two behind him briefly, but their voices had died down.

The foyer room was a wreck. The blast wave from the explosion had knocked over furniture, sending it clattering across the room. The door to the tunnel was as it was when they all entered. He rushed through it, flashlight and pistol at the ready.

The cave-in was substantial. Whomever Haggerty had

sent in obviously triggered the explosives, but how had they missed the glow sticks? He looked around, spotting one sticking out from under the rubble. It was dimmer than he'd have expected it to be.

He swore and approached the rock pile. It was gonna take forever to shift this much rock. He holstered his pistol and started.

The security door swung closed with a groan. Two men were standing inside the storage room, looking around. The lights were already on.

"You leave these on?" the shorter one asked.

The taller shook his head. "No, man. You know how mad the boss gets when we leave the lights on." His friend nodded his agreement.

The two men crept further into the room. Nothing looked out of place. The tall one waved a hand, bringing them to a stop. He pointed.

The shorter one swore under his breath, pulling a phone out of his back pocket. The phone rang twice. "Ma'am, we think we've been compromised." He listened. "No, ma'am. Yes. Yes, it was the intrusion alarm. No. Okay, sorry, yes, ma'am." He made a face at his colleague. "Yes, ma'am. We're on it." He pocketed the phone. "I shoulda made you call her."

"No way."

Neither man knew how many other pairs worked for their boss, but they knew that when the app she installed in their phones sent an alert, they dropped everything and drove out to the eastern Colorado plains.

Both knew that there wasn't a delivery scheduled to arrive, so the alert meant something else. The door at the back of the storeroom had been locked for as long as either could remember. Finding it open and the lights on was disconcerting, to say the least.

Normally, they'd arrive and head down the roughhewn tunnel to a door. On the other side of that door was always a box or two. The tunnel had a custom designed cargo mover installed in the floor, and the men would escort the packages back to the storeroom, put them on the shelf where they should go, take any packages that others had placed in specific areas, and leave. They never knew who else worked the room, never saw anyone else. The shelving that filled the room had three sections: arrivals, holdings, and outbound. Anything sitting on the outbound shelf when a team arrived was taken with them when a team left and deposited at a specific dead drop location in a commercial business park a few miles away.

"She wants us to hang tight. Reinforcements are en route." He made air quotes as he said the last part.

"What?"

"Did I stutter?"

"Shit," the taller one hissed.

The short one looked at the metal hatch that led to the tunnel they used to access the airport. As a security precaution, it was always closed and half hidden by a crate when the room was unattended. He pointed. "They didn't come through that." The hatch was still closed and the old crate was still in front of it. Likely, whoever was in there didn't even know about it.

The taller sighed. "Great."

The short one leaned to look past his friend into the room beyond. It was lit by some type of lightbulb or something stuck to the wall. He crept into the room.

His friend, still in the first room, hissed, then whispered, "So, what's it like in there?"

"You like canned peaches?"

Both men made a slow circle of the room, examining its ancient contents.

CHAPTER 9

Bryan looked at the arched doorway and stairs beyond. "What the fuck is going on?"

Sofia shushed him. "Later." She pointed to the ramp that led deeper into the facility, the way Jason, Scarlet, and Bryan had just come.

Jason motioned everyone to hurry down the ramp. He didn't know what had the ex-Marine spooked, but he knew not to question it. If she said move, he moved.

At the base of the ramp, Bryan stopped. "What the fuck is happening right now? You people need to start talking." His hand was on the butt of the pistol at his hip.

Sofia looked around, then nodded to Niles.

The natural lecturer took a breath before explaining. "We found a door cut into the wall of the second storeroom. We also found that same room full of cargo that originated around the world but all passed through Denver International Airport."

The big SPS officer looked around. "So?"

Jason inhaled. "Smugglers."

"Seems like," Sofia agreed.

"There's no way smugglers built this entire...whatever it is," Bryan said, louder than anyone else liked. He waved his hands to encompass the facility above and below them.

Sofia said, "You're right. Whoever is doing the smuggling is just using this place. They wired up a generator to power lights in that room only." She ran a hand through her close-cropped hair. "Oh, *dios mio.*"

"What?" Scarlet asked.

Sofia looked at Niles. "The door between the two rooms. They didn't even bother to come into the facility. It was still locked."

"And now it isn't," Jason surmised.

"And it's wide open," Niles groaned. The university was definitely looking better.

"And there's a stick-em in the first room." Sofia sighed.

"What?" Bryan shouted. Everyone spun to glare at him. He looked around, then physically shrunk a bit. "Sorry."

"We need to go. Put some distance between us and who is up there," Jason said. He pointed to the ramp that led deeper into the facility.

"What's down there?" Sofia asked.

Scarlet shrugged. "We didn't get very far."

Bryan turned in a slow circle. "What about Matt? Let's go back to the main tunnel. Maybe we can get through?"

Sofia put a hand on his shoulder, stopping him in his tracks. "Don't worry. This kind of shit happens to us more often than you'd guess. We'll get to the bottom of it." She tilted her head to Jason. "Jace isn't half bad with sticky situations."

Niles added, "I suspect the tunnel is now impassable. If not for us, certainly..." He inclined his head in Scarlet's direction.

Bryan blushed, then inhaled deeply, finally nodding. He now had his pistol in hand.

Scarlet led the way down the ramp, her chair's headlight lighting the way.

Niles caught up to Jason. "How many stick-ems do you have?"

Jason dropped a hand into the satchel at his side. "Not many."

The other man nodded. "Same."

As quickly as possible, Scarlet led the newly re-formed team through the rooms that she, Jason, and Bryan had already explored. They couldn't be sure whoever had been using that storeroom above wasn't looking for them.

Jason worried that the stick-ems would be a problem but weighed the value over having to work in pitch darkness with only flashlights. He passed a stick-em and continued on.

Niles slowed at the coffee table with magazines. "Oh, my. Look at these relics. So well preserved."

Sofia clucked from behind him, urging him on.

They reached another wide ramp that led down, and with a glance over her shoulder, Scarlet led the way.

Sofia had taken up the rear position, letting the others get far enough ahead that she could listen for pursuit. She heard none. Yet.

The ramp ended at a long corridor made of cinder blocks like everywhere else in the weird subterranean facility. Scarlet's headlights played down the tunnel until the gloom won. The end of the tunnel wasn't visible.

Niles moved to take the lead, his own beam of light making it no further than Scarlet's. He reached into a satchel at his side, withdrawing one of the little adhesive lights. Tapping the activation sensor, he slapped it against the cinder block wall, and the molecular adhesive did its job. The small dome wouldn't budge until turned off.

The tunnel was illuminated, but the end was still lost in the darkness.

"Damn, this is a long tunnel," Bryan said, moving further ahead of the team, his pistol at the ready. Jason joined him, both aiming their flashlights down the length of the tunnel.

Niles looked around. "This must go further east than any of the other areas we've been in."

Scarlet looked over at him, squinting. "Good spatial awareness." The academic beamed. She pointed to one of the displays at the end of the arms of her chair. A small line drawing map of the facility was visible.

"You're mapping this place?" The big man leaned down to examine the map.

Sofia joined the others. "No one coming up behind us."

Scarlet nodded at Niles. "It'd be easier with the ducklings, but my chair has a basic LiDAR mapping." She pointed to a small sphere attached to an arm just above her head.

Bryan looked over his shoulder. "I thought that was a radio antenna."

"Satellite all the way, baby," Scarlet said, patting the other arm of her chair. Realizing what she'd said and to whom, she blushed.

Jason watched the two of them, then turned to Sofia, shrugging. The ex-Marine chuckled.

"What?" Niles asked, catching the look that passed between his two friends.

Jason pointed down the tunnel. "Let's go."

"Are you fucking crazy? Is that the problem, Clark? Those years in the jungle or desert or whatever, killing people for the government—that's gone to your head?" Latricia Jackson was pacing around the perimeter of her office. She continued, "You work for a fucking airport, Clark. Not the CIA, not a third world warlord, not our government. An airport!"

JK Scheinberg and Melissa Rafferty were standing in the room's corner, trying to take up as little space as possible. Clark Haggerty was standing at military attention in the middle of the room, his gaze just over Latricia Jackson's head out her window.

The tunnel explosion had triggered alarms throughout the airport. The TSA oversight team had been on the edge of closing and evacuating the airport when JK phoned Melissa, who phoned Latricia, who was almost nose to nose with the head of the airport's head of domestic operations. The TSA woman had her finger hovering over the bright red button that would shut down the country's third busiest airport.

Seismic sensors as far south as Castlerock and as far north as Fort Lupton had registered the explosion. It had been almost three times more powerful than the first booby trap in the tunnel. Either the first one had degraded, or whoever installed the second was heavy-handed with the explosive material. No one knew which, and at the moment, it didn't matter.

Clark Haggerty, for his part, had been absorbing Latricia's ire for nearly twenty minutes. The moment she had the TSA stand down, she called that man to her office. When she stopped to take a breath, he finally said, "Are you done?"

The question caused JK and Melissa to gasp. Few people took such a tone with the amazonesque airport executive.

Latricia's eyes widened. She took a deep breath. "Momentarily."

The big mercenary squared his shoulders and said, "Okay. As you know, I answer to the mayor, same as you. This facility is operated under the governance of the city and county of Denver. Your office cuts the check, but I speak to the mayor, the same as you."

When Latricia said nothing, he continued, "Securing the terminals and baggage claim and all that bullshit is only one part of my mandate. Securing the city's investment and securing the airport proper is the other. This is the third busiest airport in America and in the top ten internationally. You think my job is just making sure knuckleheads don't bring pocketknives on their flight?"

Latricia had caught her breath and said, "So sending in your storm troopers when I had explicitly forbidden it? Just doing your job?"

He shrugged. "You wanted to bring in those California yahoos. I let you. They clearly fucked it up somehow."

"You let me?" she ground out.

He ignored the comment. "One of my people called in for backup. I responded. When the transmission cut out, I sent in reinforcements. Standard procedure."

"Which resulted in the tunnel collapsing," the airport's chief executive said.

Again, Clark shrugged. "This job isn't without risks."

"You're airport fucking security!" When he didn't respond, Latricia continued. "Your goons almost shut the airport down. Do you think the mayor would appreciate that? Would that be fulfilling your obligation?"

Clark sighed. "Look. I'm sorry. That team screwed up and paid the price." He looked over his shoulder at JK and Melissa. "Their people are trying to excavate the tunnel. See if there are any survivors. We can see what's what when that's done."

"What's what?" The statuesque executive ran a hand over her tightly bound hair. "What's what is that until you hear from me—explicitly me, from my own mouth—you and your people will stand the fuck down. Hear me?" She locked eyes with him. He held her gaze a moment before he nodded. "Good."

The door connecting the storage room to the roughhewn tunnel swung open. The two men inside spun to look at the new arrivals.

The blonde woman that both men feared more than anything, walked in. Six people in matte black combat armor, armed with automatic rifles, followed in her wake.

"Gentlemen," she said as she reached the two. "Report."

"Oh, uh..." the shorter one stammered.

She turned to the man next to him. "You're..."

"David."

She nodded. "David. Report."

David glanced at his friend quickly, then said, "Not much going on, ma'am. We took a look around the room on the other side." He motioned to the freshly opened door. "Just a bunch of old stuff. We checked out our access tunnel. It doesn't look like anyone used it. Still covered per procedure."

The scary blonde woman inclined her head. "And?"

David scuffed his boot on the ground. "Uh...that's it?" He gestured toward the now open door connecting to the rest of the facility. "There's a staircase that leads down and another secured door in that room. We...we didn't go any further."

The blonde woman turned to the six armed people. "Secure that room." She pointed through the door that, until now, she had intentionally never opened or allowed any of her people to open. She knew what the facility was and wanted nothing to do with the rest of it. This storage room was all she needed.

One of the larger reaction team members nodded.

A deep voice replied, "Yes, ma'am."

She turned back to David. "Anything else?"

David swallowed. "No. No, ma'am."

She smiled. "Good job. Stay here. Make sure no one comes this way but us." She turned to exit the storage room, following the reaction team.

The shorter man turned to his friend. "I think maybe I'll take my mom up on her offer and go work with her at the winery."

David's head bobbed in agreement. "She hiring?"

The reaction team cleared the storage room. After examining the adhesive light fixtures, they agreed they were nothing but what they seemed, and let them be. Moving down the stairs into a room full of stainless-steel shelves and work surfaces, the six-man assault force made a slow circuit around the room.

A man burst from an arched doorway at the opposite end. "Damnit. I can't raise—" He looked up just as all six armed men and women fired two shots each. Matt Jacoby hit the ground with a thud. His armor stopped many of the shots, but not all. He coughed up blood and looked at the people standing over him. Black tactical gear, assault rifles. They weren't SPS, but who?

The group parted as a blonde woman stepped into

view. "Interesting." She made a motion and stepped back. Matt tried to talk but it came out a choked gurgle. One of the bullets had struck him in the neck. The largest of the six black-clad people stepped closer and put a pistol to Matt's forehead. That was the last thing he saw.

Ms. Murphy didn't even flinch at the single gunshot. To no one in particular, she said, "That man was SPS. Airport security. They must have found a way into this facility somehow."

The team leader joined her. "Orders?"

Murphy looked around. "He was coming back from there." She pointed to the ramp leading up. "Send two of your people to recon and report back." He nodded. She added, "The rest will head down. Those two can catch up."

The big man turned to issue orders.

The dull roar of gunfire found the team. Everyone dropped to a crouch, Bryan and Sofia spinning on their heels to face the way they came, weapons raised.

"That was rifle fire," Sofia said.

Bryan nodded. "A lot of it."

No one else moved. They were still in the long dark tunnel, having taken it slowly in the dim lighting. Stick-ems were getting low in supply.

"Sounded pretty far away," Jason said. "Lot of echo. Gotta be up near the storerooms." Nods all around.

"What do you think—" Scarlet started to ask before a single gunshot interrupted her.

Sofia sighed. "That *pendejo*. Got himself killed." Bryan turned to her. She shrugged. "Sorry, *amigo*. That single shot, that was someone ending someone else." The big man scowled but nodded his agreement.

"Okay, let's keep going," Jason urged. In the gloom up ahead was a single heavy door.

Scarlet's headlights illuminated the door. The entire hallway—nearly a half kilometer, by Scarlet's measurements—was empty. One long, featureless corridor.

Jason reached for the door, pulling it open with ease.

Niles leaned over to Sofia. "I thought it'd be locked."

"Me too." She smiled.

Jason led the group through the door into another chamber similar to but also different from those they'd already explored.

"Guess we found the important section," Scarlet quipped as the group entered another circular room.

Sofia looked around the room. In the center was another ramp heading down. Between the ramp and the door they just came through was a pair of metal desks. Pre-fab room dividers acted as funnel walls, guiding anyone entering the room to the two desks.

"Security checkpoint," she said.

Bryan nodded. "Definitely."

Jason placed one of his few remaining stick-ems on the wall, bathing the chamber in thin light. He looked at the others. "I'm almost out."

Niles said, "I've got two."

"Let's keep moving," Jason said.

"Jace, surely you don't think there's a way out, deeper into this facility—whatever it is," Niles said as the group funneled between the two desks toward the ramp.

Bryan followed the Expedition, Inc. team, looking around the room. It looked a lot like the ready room SPS had up in the airport. Long benches, lockers, a few tall storage units against the wall.

Jason shrugged. "Honestly, I'm kinda just hoping something comes to me."

Sofia whistled. "I wonder if that little French scoundrel is hiring?"

Philippe Bouchard had moved to the top of the ex-Marine's shit list after he slipped away from the authorities on Graham Island. The little weasel had triggered the destruction of the secret Japanese base, and almost all of its contents, in his attempt to secure it for his wealthy backer. In the end, what should have been a historical find for the centuries was little more than a crater in an island no one had heard of until the military swarmed it.

Jason looked at her, eyebrow raised.

"Just thinking out loud," she said, smiling. "You know I'd just as soon stab him as work for him."

Jason grunted and moved toward the ramp in the floor. "This place sure has a weird layout."

Scarlet rolled up behind him, pointing to her wire-frame map. "I honestly haven't been able to figure out a pattern. We're several hundred feet below ground now and almost a kilometer east of the main terminal buildings. One section is a single room; others have more than one."

Niles said, "Add to that, these ramps." He smiled to Scarlet. "It's good they're here, but why?"

Bryan said, "Accessibility?"

Scarlet barked a laugh. "Half the sidewalks in San Diego aren't accessible. There's no way someone was paying that much attention to it back in the '90s." The big man frowned but nodded his agreement.

The group headed down the ramp.

As a kid, Elizabeth Murphy had never intended to work for organized crime, let alone reach a place of prominence in one of the world's largest, and least known, syndicates.

As the child of prominent heart surgeons in the Kensington neighborhood of London, the young towheaded child was expected to follow in her parents' footsteps.

Life had other plans for the young aristocrat. Her boarding school roommate had been the daughter of the prominent businessman, and member of the Ten Dragons, Walter Kang. The two became inseparable.

Chloe and Elizabeth were on holiday before university when a hit squad from a rival organization attempted to kidnap Chloe. Elizabeth fought off the attackers, then concocted a plan to not just evade the attackers but take them out.

Walter Kang had been impressed with the young woman's ruthless brutality and calculating mind. Elizabeth's career trajectory changed forever.

The reaction team leader cleared his throat. "Ma'am, the two men I sent into the tunnel are back."

Ms. Murphy shook her head to clear her thoughts. "And?"

"Collapsed. Whatever explosive was used was powerful, probably too much so. It'll be days, likely weeks, before anyone can clear it."

"And it led right into the facility?" The big man nodded. "I see. That's good. Maybe this entire thing is salvageable." She inclined her head toward the door in front of the team. "I guess we continue deeper into this bizarre rabbit hole."

The big man turned but stopped when she put a hand on his shoulder. "Erickson, no one leaves this place that isn't us." He nodded.

Beyond the doorway was a long, sparsely lit tunnel. About halfway down its length, she could see one of the strange adhesive light fixtures.

Whomever she and her men were pursuing, they had some interesting toys.

Erickson barked orders to his people. The six formed pairs: two in front, one on either side of Murphy, and two in the rear.

Walking through the tunnel, Murphy's thoughts drifted back to Chloe Kang, her best friend and boss. Walter Kang died two years after the women graduated from Oxford. With Elizabeth's help, Chloe had eliminated the two men vying to take over Walter's chapter of the organization. The two women had been thick as thieves ever since.

It was only when Elizabeth had read about the various rumors surrounding Denver International Airport, and done some digging of her own, that she pitched the idea to Chloe. The Ten Dragons could double, if not triple, their export business if they could get around customs. The rumored secret facilities around Denver International Airport, if they existed and she could find them, would be the perfect means to that end.

Her quest started with looking for people who might have worked construction around the time the airport was being built but weren't on airport payroll. It had taken over a year to find a solid lead.

PART THREE

The ramp ended at a short corridor, and at the end of that corridor was another door.

"This is new," Niles said. The door had a label. In blocky white letters, it read COMMAND/RESIDEN-TIAL. Next to the door was a stool and a lectern.

"This has to be some sort of military facility," Sofia said. "That was a ready room and checkpoint up above, and this," she pointed to the lectern, "is another checkpoint."

"Whose?" Jason asked, half serious.

Scarlet said, "Gotta be some type of shelter. Right? I mean, it says command and residential."

Niles sighed. "One way to find out." He reached for the door.

"Is that a—" Bryan objected.

Niles pushed the door open. "Good idea?" He swept his flashlight around the room. "Well, now."

Sofia and Jason followed. "Damn," the former said.

The wide circular space was larger than any they had seen yet, easily three stories tall. A wide circular walkway ringed the entire space about halfway up, creating a second level. From across the large cavern, they could see dormant computer terminals and at least one or two of what must have been office doors on the second level. To one side was a metal framed circular staircase connecting the two floors.

A raised platform in the center held a large table. The outer perimeter of the ground floor, like the one above, was lined with workstations and computer terminals. Occasionally, a door broke the pattern, a nameplate next to each one.

Niles moved his flashlight around the space. Whatever the facility was, it had remained a secret for decades under the Colorado plains. Documenting a find of this magnitude would be a labor of months, if not years, and would keep him in academic papers for as long. Not to mention the work he still had lined up as a result of the Canada job. How could he walk away from something like that?

"This stuff is ancient," Scarlet said, rolling toward the nearest desk. There was a keyboard and mouse accompanied by a monitor almost as deep as it was wide. She looked under the desk to spot the location a PC would be situated. Nothing.

She looked around. For whatever reason, the people that set the facility up hadn't installed the computers—at least most of the computers. A few desks seemed to have an ancient tower computer with the logo of a company long since defunct, under them.

The others made their way to the center of the room.

Stepping up onto the raised platform, Jason saw that the tabletop was a map of the United States. Tucked into a small compartment were little plastic pieces painted red, blue, green, and yellow.

"What the..." Niles wondered aloud when he joined his friend.

Bryan stepped up next to the pair. He turned a slow circle. "This is a military command center." He turned back to the table, pointing to the bits of colored plastic. "Missiles. Or maybe impacts. The colors would mark confirmed and suspected impacts."

"What gave it away?" Sofia deadpanned from where she was looking through the drawers of one of the desks.

"Aziz, light!" Scarlet shouted. A loud clack followed her proclamation, followed by nothing.

She had moved to a section of the curved wall devoid of workstations. Two large switchgears were both in the up or "on" position. The panel they were mounted to was outlined in yellow and black warning tape.

"Was something supposed to happen?" Sofia asked.

Everyone was staring at her. Scarlet reached up and awkwardly pulled both switchgears down. She looked over her shoulder. "Once more with feeling. Aziz, light!" She pushed both switches up, locking them into position with loud clacks. Still nothing. Mumbling under her breath, she pulled at each switch, dusting off the contacts, blowing on them, pushing and pulling, testing the hinges. She pushed a few switches up and down.

"Who is Aziz?" Sofia asked.

Bryan smiled. "From the movie, *The Fifth Element*."

Sofia stared at him. The big blond opened his mouth to explain, but she waved a hand, making a buzzing sound. "She makes me watch movies. We're green." The two shared a chuckle while Jason sighed.

Scarlet pushed one of the switchgears up. This time when the two metal bars struck the bracket, a burst of sparks erupted from the switch. Several indicators under the switch lit up.

"Yes!" She repeated the process with the other switch, slamming it home.

From nowhere in particular, a low hum began to build.

Bryan looked around. "Uh, that was maybe not a good idea?"

"Don't be a wuss," Scarlet scolded, rolling toward the raised dais. The hum continued to build. Overhead, fluorescent light fixtures that gently curved along the domed ceiling flickered to life. Many of them strobed and then remained dark. Several others went from a dim glow to fully illuminated as ancient argon and mercury were exposed to current. Eventually, more than half the decades-old light bars came to life and remained lit, bathing the space in harsh white light.

Everyone shielded their eyes. They'd been in the dark for several hours with only flashlights and stick-ems for light.

Around the perimeter, monitors flickered to life and computers beeped as they powered up. Hard drives that had not been used in decades clattered as they booted up.

"They must have wired this place directly into the

airport's grid," Niles surmised. He looked around once more. "This is…Jason, this is unbelievable."

Jason wondered what the airport's power plant manager was likely thinking, watching his power consumption suddenly jump.

Scarlet laughed. "Holy shit."

Everyone turned to her again.

She shook her head, adjusting her ponytail. "Back when they were building the airport, it kept falling behind schedule—to the tune of months, by the end, almost a year. No one could ever explain the delay, but it had to be this. The government must have built this while the airport was being built. No one would have really been able to tell the difference between this project and the terminal buildings and runways."

"And since it was just an airport, there wasn't much scrutiny or press coverage," Niles said. He was still digesting what he was seeing and what it meant.

Jason nodded. "Makes sense. I mean, as far as secret government facilities go." He looked around. "But why?"

"Continuity of government," Sofia offered.

Bryan, rubbing the back of his neck, said, "She's right. The government woulda wanted a place to relocate in the event of a nuclear war." He looked around. "Cheyenne Mountain would make sense, but even then, it was too well known. Everyone knew about that fancy joint in West Virginia. They needed someplace else, secret."

Before the group could discuss the historical basis for the facility, voices drifted through the door to the ramp leading back up to the security checkpoint. One of them was distinctly British.

Misty and her team were walking back to the team lounge, their shift over. Finally. Three FedEx 929s had come in at the same time, full.

Whatever that explosion was had resulted in a short ground stop, which only further delayed things.

An aircraft marshaller came around the corner. "Hey, guys. You feel that explosion earlier?"

"How could we not?" Misty replied. "You hear anything about it? They didn't close this place down for long, so..."

The marshaller shook his head. "Not much. I heard some gate agents talking a while ago that something happened out where they're doing that new cargo expansion."

Rodrigo Martinez looked at Misty, then the marshaller. "Something explode?"

"I guess they found something down there." He shrugged. "One of the gals over at D32 said it was a missile silo. Another said it was a military base that no one is using. I guess the one gal has been dating one of the construction folks."

"Maybe it's smugglers," Misty offered. The two men turned to her, Rodrigo's mouth hung open. The marshaller had a blank look on his face. "You know, like drugs and exotic animals and stuff." She could feel sweat beading on her forehead. She did not know what made her say it. "I dunno, just throwing it out there." She pointed behind the marshaller in the direction she and the others were originally heading. "We gotta go."

In the break room, as the team shed orange reflective vests, hard hats, and other gear, one of the other men on the team, Joe Gilroy, leaned over. "What did you mean, smuggling?"

The muscles in Misty's neck tensed. She was leaning over, tying her sneaker. She didn't look up. "What? Oh, back there. Uh, nothing." It came out as much a statement as a question.

The other man sat on the bench. "I just ask because, well..." His face was crimson as he trailed off.

Misty looked sideways at him. "It wouldn't be hard to set up a smuggling operation if you had some type of underground facility connected to the cargo terminal."

Her heart was pounding. She couldn't come out and admit what she was doing, but hoped that if Joe was in the same situation, he'd pick up on what she was saying.

He looked over, taking a breath. "Yeah, a door no one really pays attention to, somewhere in the lower levels..." He again let the last few words out as whispers.

"You leave a piece of cargo there, it could vanish," she snapped her fingers, "like that. No one would notice."

"You too?" he asked. Sweat was running down his temple. Misty nodded. "Jesus Christ, I thought it was just me."

"So did I," she admitted.

The two looked around, ensuring no one was within earshot, and told each other their stories.

After confirming that their experiences, down to the polite and terrifying British woman, matched, they headed off to find someone to tell.

Jason looked at the door they had come through, then around the wide, circular space. There was one door opposite the one they came in though that stood out from the others that lined the command center. For one thing, it was a double door made of wood. For another, the block letter paint spelled out RESIDENTIAL across both doors.

He nodded toward the doors. Everyone hustled toward them.

Pushing through the doors, Jason let out a low whistle. His flashlight beam fell across coffee tables, sofas, and chairs, all covered in a fine carpet of dust. Like most of the rooms in the facility, the residential room was circular, with doors at regular intervals all the way around.

Niles looked around. It would seem that only the command center warranted over nine-foot ceilings. He had no doubt that anyone trapped in this bunker for longer than a year would develop crippling claustrophobia.

The others filed in behind Jace, snapping their flashlights on before playing them around the room. Jason felt around until he found a light switch, assuming that power was now flowing to this room as well, thanks to Scarlet.

Fluorescent light strips flickered to life as flashlights clicked off again.

Directly opposite the team was a door that was not like the others.

"Is that the—" Scarlet asked, rolling up next to Jason.

"The seal of the President of the United States? Yeah," he answered.

Lit by a strategically placed light fixture, a dark oak door stood closed. Looking like it had just been hung on the door was a plaque with the seal of the President, the paint crisp and bright.

From behind the pair, Niles turned to Bryan and Sofia, then Jason and Scarlet. "Guess that answers that."

"Holy shit," Bryan whispered. "How are you all not freaking out? I'm freaking out. I mean," he pointed to the door, "that's where the President would ride out a nuclear war."

Jason smiled. "We're used to weird stuff like this." He shrugged. "This one might take the cake, though."

Niles nodded. In a low, almost reverential, voice, he said, "And it never gets old."

Sofia added, "They planned to run whatever was left of the country out of here. Makes sense to have a place to sleep."

Bryan ran a hand through his hair, sending dust in every direction. "Why put the residential area behind the command center?" He looked around. "Seems like the bunk rooms shoulda been up there somewhere." He waved in the general direction of the facility they had already explored above them.

"All the people with guns would be between the front door and the President," Sofia offered.

Niles nodded his agreement. "Likely everyone allowed into this bunker would be of value and possess sufficient clearance, so restricting access wouldn't matter."

Bryan thought that over and nodded.

Scarlet shook her head. "All those conspiracy nuts over the last twenty-thirty years. They were right."

Sofia turned to her. "Aren't they usually?"

Niles clucked.

Jason cleared his throat. "Okay, we're not in the clear. Anything but." He gestured around the room's perimeter. "Check all these. I'm guessing they're bunks, but let's be sure. We've still got bad guys behind us; let's make sure we know the lay of the land." Everyone spread out, checking doors, poking their heads into rooms.

Jason strode across the room, dodging furniture until he was right in front of the oak door. Taking a deep breath, he pushed it open. "Woah."

Jason jumped as Sofia pushed him out of the way as she walked into the room. "Hot damn." She whistled.

"What happened to clearing the other rooms?"

The ex-Marine waved a hand. "They got it." She moved deeper into the room.

The room was the same size as the rest of the rooms being investigated by the others, except that instead of bunks, there was a large conference table with seating for twelve in the room's front. It was immaculate, adorned in dark woods and brushed metals. The fluorescent lighting of the command center was absent. Wall sconces and floor lamps lit the room in warm light. In the northwest corner, a desk of deep red wood with a brass lamp on its corner sat under the familiar layer of dust. Hung on the wall over the desk was the seal of the President of the United States.

A pre-fab wall divided the room, keeping a bed and other creature comforts out of view.

Jason pointed at the opening in the pre-fab divider. "Must be the President's private suite, back there."

"Probably," Niles agreed as he joined Jason and Sofia. He hitched a thumb. "I think I found the VP's room. Not nearly as opulent, but not bad either." He was holding a book he'd picked up from a nightstand in the room, *Tom Sawyer*.

"Nice enough to ride out a nuclear winter?" Scarlet asked from behind them.

Niles clucked. "Lord, no."

Bryan dropped into one of the seats around the conference table, a cloud of fine dust erupting around him. He looked at the Expedition, Inc. team. "So, uh, now what?"

Sofia looked back the way they had come. "This is a dead end. We're out of rooms."

Jason sighed. "Alamo time, I guess?" He moved to the conference table, joining Bryan and motioning the others over. He eased himself into a seat, hoping to not cause a dust eruption. He was not successful.

After pulling a chair out of the way to make room,

Scarlet rolled up to the table, placing a tablet down on the tabletop. "Sorry, this is all I got. No Wi-Fi down here."

"Or displays that would even know what that means," Sofia quipped.

Scarlet inclined her head. "There's that." She pointed to the tablet. On the screen was a rough outline of the facility, created by her chair's mapping capabilities. She pointed. "We're here."

Niles squinted. "That?" He pointed.

"No. Here." She pointed, tapping the screen. "The one that looks like a big important room."

"Oh. I see," he said, glancing at Sofia and shrugging.

Scarlet sighed. "Anyway." Her finger traced a path. "If we can get back up to the security foyer, we can use that as our first line of defense."

Bryan looked around. "You all are serious?" When no one answered, he continued, "I have my sidearm and this." He shifted in his seat to pull the compact machine gun around from behind him on the strap. He looked around the table, gaze settling on Sofia. "You've got a pistol?" She nodded. He looked at Jason, who did the same.

"Yeah, we're super not equipped for last stands. At least not the kind that ends well for us," Jason said.

Scarlet raised a hand. "Uh, excuse me. Ableist much?"

"What?"

"You didn't ask me if I had a weapon."

Bryan sighed and hitched a thumb at Niles. "I didn't ask him either. Nerds usually aren't armed. No offense."

Niles tilted his head, nodding fractionally.

"I resent that comment," Scarlet scoffed. "And you'd

be wrong." She grinned, baring her teeth and holding up something that looked kind of like a ray gun.

"What's that?" Bryan asked, crossing his arms over his chest.

"Stunner." The look on his face killed her giant grin. "Not unarmed," she said under her breath. Niles put a reassuring hand on her shoulder.

Bryan shook his head. "Anyway. Not to harp on our situation, but we heard their voices. Getting back up to the security foyer is out of the question."

Jason nodded. "He's right. On both counts. We need to come up with a way to get around them. I figure we've got maybe five minutes before they're in the command center. Maybe ten more before they come through those doors." He pointed out through the door to the Presidential suite, to the double doors that connected the residential and command center rooms.

His gaze moved to each person. "Ideas?"

Latricia Jackson had meant what she said to Clark Haggerty. After she caught her breath from dressing the ex-military man down and sending him away, she called the airport police chief. Normally, he and his people were relegated to guiding traffic on the arrival and departure decks and making any actual arrests SPS required.

When the TSA pulled up stakes, airport police were one of the things the mayor had cut as a first resort to stem the budgetary bleeding when they brought on SPS. She asked for as many officers as he could spare to guard the construction entrance to the cargo expansion dig site. She did not trust Clark Haggerty to follow her instructions, even a little.

She didn't have any illusions about whether the airport cops could do anything to slow down, let alone stop, Clark's SPS goons when he ignored her orders, but she'd at least know when it happened.

One of the first things SPS did when it became Denver International Airport's security contractor was to annex several offices and conference rooms in the administrative building, converting them into a sprawling command center and recreational space for the exclusive use of its officers and agents.

The recreational portion was larger than anyone would have guessed; a massive workout area filled one corner, and a kitchen area occupied the opposite corner, with lounge space in the middle. A row of lockers and weapon racks filled the remaining wall.

The other half of the space was a wall of monitors with half a dozen desks with their own computers on them, all monitoring every camera in and around the airport.

A short, wiry woman walked in to find Clark Haggerty at the table in the kitchen area. "Sir?"

He looked up, rubbing a hand across his face, setting the tablet in his other hand down. "What is it, Jones?"

The small woman cleared her throat. "Sir, I..."

Haggerty sighed. "Spit it out."

"Sir, I think there's a way into the dig site."

"That bitch Jackson has the airport cops down in the construction site." On his way to the SPS barracks, as it was called, he had sent one of his people down to take a look.

Jones coughed. "Yes, sir. I was in the security office, and a couple of cargo movers came in a little bit ago. They were both babbling excitedly about a secret door and being coerced by an evil British woman. It took a while to get them to slow down and explain, and—"

"Spit it out, Jones," Haggerty growled, slamming his palm on the table. He stood up and went to the refrigerator. He grabbed a soda and took a long swig.

She cleared her throat. "Sorry, sir, yes, sir. Anyway, it seems that someone has been using the airport employees to smuggle cargo into and out of the airport. Apparently, for a few years. These two idiots, and who knows how many others, get a text with the details, and then they move a piece of cargo down to the sub-level of the cargo terminal. I guess there's a door there or something. They just park the cargo and leave."

"And then what?" He tossed the soda bottle into the recycling bin. What was Jones going on about? Smuggling? Airport employees? There was no way a smuggling operation was running under his nose. It was impossible. He didn't have time to figure out whatever it was that she was going on about. Whatever was going on underground was far more important; he could feel it.

Jones shuffled her feet. "Well, they didn't know. Sir."

She met his gaze and looked down. "They said that they'd park the cargo mover and leave it. By the time they came around that area again, the cargo would be gone." She met Clark's eyes. "It's gotta be related to whatever this whole thing is, right? Maybe there's a way to get down there, save Matt and Bryan."

Haggerty said nothing. If this was related and if there was a way to get down into whatever was beyond the dig site, he could destroy it or close it down. Whatever he had to do in order to restore order and get the airport back to normal.

"Sir?"

He held up a hand. "Get a team out here from the Fort Collins office. Now."

The small woman nodded and darted over to one of the desks, turning the laptop on it around toward her.

SPS had offices all along the front range, handling all manner of security-related needs.

Clark rubbed his chin. Latricia Jackson was going to ruin the airport with this nonsense. Letting those squints from California go down there nearly unsupervised was her first horrible decision, one that caused death and further delays of the cargo annex expansion. He lost seven good men and women already and would be damned if he'd let her put his company's annual bonus in jeopardy. Her second mistake had been excluding him from any further decisions around whatever it was that was under the airport.

Part of SPS's contract with the airport was bonuses tied to the airport's overall financial performance. Every minute the California yahoos were keeping the new cargo facility from being completed, he could feel this quarter's bonus evaporating. It was already bad enough he'd had so many deaths on his watch, but SPS carried excellent corporate insurance for just such occasions. Missing one or more bonuses would be a disaster.

He turned to Jones. "I'll meet the team outside. Get me more details on this door or whatever it is. Where, how, all of it. Send it to my phone."

She looked up and nodded, then turned her attention back to the video call with the Fort Collins office.

Clark Haggerty walked out of the break room and toward the nearest exit to the employee parking structure.

The Ten Dragons' fast reaction team walked out of the armory as the lights strung along the ceiling flickered to life.

All together, they dropped into combat-ready crouches, rifles at the ready. Elizabeth Murphy, in the middle of the formation, looked around. "Interesting."

Nothing more happened. The team relaxed, straightening up, rifles still at the ready.

Murphy turned to the strike team leader. "These people are clever."

"They'll die all the same, ma'am," the big man said, motioning his team toward the ramp leading deeper into the structure.

Oracle was impressed, or the artificial intelligence version of what impressed would feel like. She would have to ask Scarlet about it later. The airport's computer systems were remarkably well protected. She did not have a frame of reference, having avoided accessing any federally controlled systems, at Scarlet's urging, until now, but even so, she had expected it to be easier.

The systems aboard the *Peregrine* were good, but not as powerful as those back in San Diego or even aboard the *Raven*. In order to continue forcing her way into the airport's systems, Oracle shifted as many secondary processes as she could to the equipment back home to free up local resources. It wasn't optimal, but most of the processes she shifted could handle the lag inherent in crossing a thousand miles.

It took two hours of gentle probing for her to penetrate the airport's computer systems. Approximately one hundred and thirty-two percent longer than she thought it should have taken.

Once inside, she was able to isolate every department within the airport: food services, administrative, air traffic control, baggage handling, and security. Two security departments, in fact: one with basic, almost non-existent defensive firewalls, and another that resisted her initial probes.

Interesting.

The second set of security servers were considerably newer and ran more advanced software than any other part of the airport. She withdrew her probes. She did not want to tip anyone off to her presence in the airport systems. Not yet.

She examined the air traffic control systems servers. Not relevant to her needs.

She examined the personnel management servers. Not relevant to her needs.

She examined the cargo management division servers. This was the department that hired Scarlet and the others. She dug deeper.

The airport handled thousands of pieces of cargo a day, from mail that the postal service subcontracted to cargo firms, to international shipping of anything from pet beds to tractors and everything in between. The dataset was enormous. She shifted more subroutines back to San Diego in order to parse the immense set of data from the cargo management system. She wouldn't need her proximity and visual scanning systems. The hangar had been empty for hours after she chased those two interlopers off.

She didn't know what she was looking for, but somewhere in the cargo department's data were details on her friends and the project that they had been hired for. She would need more local processing power to parse the data on those servers.

Outside the *Peregrine,* the men from before opened the door to the hangar. One leaned in. "Still there."

The other stepped in, followed by three others. "Joey, Marcus, Malik. That's it." The man gestured to the matte black plane that had chased him and his friend out of the hangar a few hours back.

"That the plane that scared you, Timmy?" the biggest of the three, Malik, said.

"Whatever, man. Let's get it opened up before that little one attacks." Timmy waved his friend in. "Come on, John!"

John let the door close behind him slowly. The weird black plane was sitting exactly where it was when he and Timmy had found it earlier.

After being chased off by that weird drone thing, they lay low in case airport security showed up. When nothing happened, they called some friends.

Timmy and John worked maintenance in the private hangar area of the airport. They had been breaking into private planes for years, taking odds and ends that they could easily get away with. The area was not very well guarded by SPS goons.

Marcus and Joey crept toward the plane. The former whispered, "You said that little attack drone thing, it came from on top?"

The other man nodded.

Inside the *Peregrine,* Oracle was reviewing the construction blueprints for the new cargo annex. Then she found the incident report for the accident with the earth mover.

An alert popped up in her consciousness, routed through San Diego. Her proximity alarm. Someone was outside.

Setting aside her research, she reprioritized proximity and visual processing.

Them again.

She pulled more processing power back into local resources, running a quick diagnostic and powering up key systems, including *Emmet*.

You brought friends.

She watched two of the men creep around under one of the plane's wings, carrying something between them.

For the nineteenth time, Oracle wished Scarlet had brought Rufus along. The mechanical automaton would be really useful right now. She would have to make do with *Emmet*.

The plane's engines spun up. On her cameras she saw the two men from before climbing on top of the fuselage. The other three moved away from the plane and the whining engines.

Oracle slid open the topside hatch over *Emmet*'s docking port. After initiating the drone's launch sequence, nothing happened.

Error F-291.

Switching to *Emmet*'s camera, she saw nothing but darkness. Even docked, the drone's camera should see light.

She accessed Scarlet's manual for the drone. Error F-291, launch failure, unable to depart.

Whatever those men had carried to the plane's top was covering the drone's docking port.

Two of the men moved to the boarding ramp, crowbars in hand.

"This thing is ridiculous," Marcus complained, wiping sweat from his brow. The seam between the ramp and the rest of the plane's fuselage was deformed where the crowbar had been used. The ramp itself, however, had not budged and didn't look like it was going to.

"You need to work out more," Malik joked from under the left wing.

Oracle watched through the cameras, unsure what to do. Without *Emmet*, she lacked a physical presence to enact her wishes.

The black SUV pulled up in front of Clark. He watched silently as five men got out. Each was in a matte black tactical jumpsuit, a pistol on each hip and an FN P98 submachine gun in each hand. Standard SPS field gear.

"Five?"

The driver of the SUV inclined his sandy-blond-haired head. "Sorry, sir. Teams 1 and 3 are still up north on the Scarborough job."

Clark remembered that job. He had an email about it somewhere. He cursed himself for forgetting, but the Colorado Springs office would have taken too long to get teams to the airport, anyway. He nodded. "Let's go."

The six men walked back into the airport administration building, through winding hallways and tunnels out to the cargo terminal.

As the group left the elevator at the lowest level of the airport, Clark's phone beeped.

Looking at it, he smiled. Jones came through. He

might have to put her in for a promotion. On the small screen was a full notes file packed with details. The names of the two airport employees, the location of the mystery door and the last time they used it were all there.

The six men walked more or less right to the door that no one had ever seen open, let alone gone through.

It looked like the description Jones provided: nondescript, no visible locks on this side, no placard showing what the door was for or where it led.

"What's this?" the team leader asked.

"Our way in," Clark replied. He looked at the surrounding men. "Let's get to work."

The team lead nodded to one of his subordinates, who slid a long pry bar out of a sheath across his back.

While the team worked the door, Clark watched. If this was some kind of smuggling operation, they had someone else inside the airport. Someone that could get this door installed, and signed off on.

He leaned over the shoulder of the nearest man. The door didn't stand out, at all.

A loud crack broke his reverie. The team leader stood, patting another man's shoulder. "We're in, sir."

The door swung open without a sound. Clark nodded, impressed. Wouldn't want anyone down here to hear a door open.

The tunnel inside wasn't what Clark expected. Thin light bars led off into the distance, and a narrow pair of tracks followed the light strips. Of the device that ran on the tracks, there was no sign.

Clark nodded to his men and women. "Let's go." He entered the tunnel.

Unlike the tunnel the construction team found, this one wasn't reinforced with cinder blocks, nor was it, as far as he could see, booby-trapped.

"Sir, what is all this?" one of the team, a short, dark-skinned woman he remembered hiring a year ago. She was ex-Navy and great with small arms, if he recalled correctly. Taylor, her name was.

"A fucking cluster, that's what, Taylor. This," he waved to the tunnel they were creeping through, "is apparently the tool of an ongoing smuggling operation." He sighed at the acknowledgment of his failure. "The cargo project found a tunnel, I guess..." he did some math and rough spatial translations in his head, "about half a kilometer southeast of here. Old, built by someone with skills; reinforced walls, that kind of thing."

The woman nodded. "Weird."

"Inconvenient is more like it."

Up ahead, the team leader held a fist in the air. Everyone stopped where they were.

"I'm not sure this idea is any better," Scarlet groused. She was parked next to a crouching Niles and Jason in the bunk room to the right of the Presidential suite. Through the barely ajar door, they could see the door that connected the living quarters to the command center.

Niles looked over. "You'd prefer to charge them,

waving your stunner?" This was the part of being with the team that he liked the least. He never had to hide at the university, at least not from armed opponents. He certainly never feared for his life. The exploration was exhilarating, the life and death stakes less so. He clutched the dusty copy of *Tom Sawyer*, prepared to hurl it at the first international criminal syndicate goon he saw.

Scarlet wobbled her head, mimicking her friend in a high-pitched voice.

Jason shushed them both.

In the room immediately to the left of the Presidential quarters, Sofia and Bryan were crouched at their own slightly ajar door.

The wait wasn't long for the armed men that they all expected to arrive. Sofia watched the six men enter the command center. She was a bit surprised to see a well-dressed and beautiful blonde-haired woman follow the mercenary squad into the space. The armed men and women fanned out, protecting the woman.

"She's cute," Bryan whispered.

"I'll tell Scarlet you said that," Sofia replied. The other man spluttered as quietly as possible. Finally, she placed a hand on his arm. "I'm kidding. And yes, yes, she is." She sighed. "Probably evil, too."

"Definitely evil," the big blond ex-Army Ranger agreed. In the entry to the residential block, the blonde was taking in the large space and issuing orders.

The five of them watched from their barely open doors as the seven newcomers did the same thing they had: spread out to look into and clear the many rooms lining the big common area. Three each went to the doors immediately to the side of the entry. The blonde stayed near the door.

The two trios came back to the woman to report that the bunk rooms were empty. As they were about to move to the next rooms, the sound of muffled voices caught everyone's attention.

The blonde woman motioned her people back to her, and as a group, they crept straight toward the Presidential suite and the sound of muffled discussion.

Two of the armed bad guys reached the doors to the Presidential suite. Pushing the doors open, the conversation that drew them to the room stopped. One looked over her shoulder to their boss. The blonde nodded. First two, then all four, commandos entered the suite.

From their respective rooms nearby, the Expedition, Inc. team watched anxiously. When it was clear that the blonde wasn't going to follow her team, Jason sighed. They had only a minute or two for those six well-armed men and women to clear the room and find the small music player behind the bed.

Before Jason could signal her, Sofia came to the same conclusion. She eased open the door to Bryan's and her room.

The two side rooms were well within the woman's peripheral vision. She'd see Sofia's door opening any second. Jason coughed.

The blonde spun toward the door that Jason, Scarlet, and Niles were crouched behind.

Scarlet turned to look at Jason, shock etched across her

face. He held a finger to his lips and then looked to Niles, who nodded as he dabbed sweat from his brow.

While the blonde woman crept toward Jason's bunk room, Sofia finished easing open the door. She and Bryan had spent several minutes once the plan was agreed on, opening and closing the door to warm up the decades-old hinges to minimize their squeaking. It worked, more or less. The door barely squeaked as it came to a stop.

Sofia looked at Bryan, catching his eyes. She pointed to herself, then to the blond. Then she pointed to him and then to the doors to the Presidential suite. He frowned, but nodded.

Without a sound, Sofia left her concealment and darted towards her target. Bryan was hot on her heels, though not nearly as quietly. The blonde woman was turning toward the noise as Sofia tackled her.

The strike team must have found the radio. Bryan could hear them speaking at a normal volume and getting louder. Closer to the doors. He reached the double doors and hefted a piece of metal, one of several they had placed near the doors ahead of time.

As he slid the thick piece of metal through the two door handles, the doors shook.

Sofia and the blonde woman stuck the concrete, hard. The blonde released a loud breath, the wind forced from her lungs. In a fluid motion, Sofia rolled off her opponent before the woman had a chance to grab onto her.

Bryan slid another piece of metal through the door handles as the doors shook. Loud shouts came from inside.

When the shouting stopped, he stepped aside. The sound of bullets striking the door filled the space. The door, at least his side of it, looked none the worse for the wear, having been shot a dozen times. He looked at the doors, eyebrows raised. "Nice." He grabbed a third piece of metal and slid it into place.

While the team had waited for their pursuers, they had scrounged a few pieces of thick metal from one of the bunk rooms. The pieces were long enough to reach through the door handles and span the door frame. It would take a lot to break through.

The rest of the team appeared in their doorway as the blonde nimbly flipped herself back to her feet to square off with Sofia.

Scarlet rolled up behind her. A blue aura surrounded the woman as every nerve in her body misfired. She twitched, then crumpled to the ground.

"I had her," Sofia grated. She cracked the knuckles of each hand.

Scarlet shrugged. "Sorry. I'll let you kick her ass next time." She smiled.

"We do have a bit of a time constraint," Niles pointed out.

Sofia and Jason reached down to lift the woman.

Scarlet rolled back toward the room she and the others had hidden in, pushing open the door.

A few minutes of tying the blonde woman to a bed and the group was ready to exit the residential section of the bunker.

Over the sound of shouts and bangs against the Presidential suite door, Jason said, "Okay, we should get going. I doubt that'll hold forever."

More bullets struck the inside of the double doors, doing little to no damage. Had the bunker ever been needed, the President would have been quite safe behind those doors.

Jason looked around. "Ready?"

Niles turned a slow circle, taking more pictures with his phone. He had already made a slow circuit of the space and the bunk rooms, taking pictures and video of every nook and cranny. Jason guessed he was worried the whole thing would fall into a pit full of water any minute. He couldn't blame him. That happened to them a lot. His own phone had quite a few pictures of the Presidential suite decor and artifacts. The satchel that had held stick-ems was now full of historic tchotchkes.

While the intruders continued their work, Oracle processed her options. She was still connected to the airport's network. Nothing in the terminal would help her, so she pulled back a bit to the local access point through which she had gained entry.

She browsed the available nodes on the network, but nothing looked promising. Until...Fire suppression. That had promise.

A loud thunk reverberated through the plane's fuselage. Oracle examined the cameras to see a pair of feet standing on the nose of the plane. There wasn't a camera in the cockpit, but she assumed one of her new friends was attempting to smash the cockpit glass to gain entry.

Unsure if it would be enough, but aware that she had few other options, Oracle took action.

The lights in the hangar shut off before the red emergency lighting activated. The intruders stopped their various attacks momentarily.

From a couple of dozen emitters in the ceiling, fire suppression foam fell. The men shouted and cursed as foam accumulated around their feet, covering every square inch of the hangar.

Oracle overrode the automatic cut off. The foam continued to fall.

The man on the nose of the plane lost his footing and fell to the ground. One of the men on top of the plane likewise lost his footing. He landed in a heap, a pile of canvas draping over him.

She accessed *Emmet* again; this time, the drone's camera showed a mix of light and what was likely foam. She attempted to activate the drone. Through the drone's camera she saw foam spray in all directions as the four propellers spun up. The view slowly rose as *Emmet* gained altitude. Foam was being flung in all directions as it landed on the drone. She disengaged the fire suppression system.

Back on the local network, several system flags were raised. Local fire control personnel were dispatched. She should have thought of this sooner. She dug through the local network until she found the smart locks on the personnel door. Locked.

The men slipped and tripped their way to the door and found it locked.

Using the small speaker built into *Emmet*, Oracle said, "YOU WILL LEAVE THIS PLACE. YOU WILL TELL NO ONE WHAT HAPPENED HERE."

"What the?" Joey demanded. His hand was still on the door handle. He jerked and twisted with all his might; the door wouldn't budge.

"I HAVE SUMMONED THE AUTHORITIES," the voice boomed from every speaker inside the cabin. The intruders did not need to know that she was shading the truth.

"YOU HAVE LESS THAN FIVE MINUTES."

"Bullshit," John said.

"JOHN BROWER. TIMOTHY JENKINS." With access to the airport's network, searching personnel files using stills from her various cameras, it had been easy to identify two of her attackers.

The two men looked at each other. "How the fuck does it know who we are?"

Emmet dove at the men, sending them scattering.

"THREE MINUTES."

The would-be thieves looked at each other, then at the plane and the drone buzzing overhead.

"Let us out and we won't come back!" Malik shouted.

The only way to know that authorities were near was by tapping into their comms. When she was relatively certain the airport police and fire were outside, Oracle released her control over the local systems, withdrawing back into the *Peregrine*'s systems. She unlocked the door and watched the men flood out of the hangar.

Before the authorities entered, she returned *Emmet* to its docking station and closed up the hatch. While the authorities cleared the hangar and walked around the unusual plane, she resumed her search for the team.

The group left the residential area and the loud banging and intermittent gunfire behind. It broke Niles's heart to think of the damage being done to those rooms. The command center looked exactly as they had left it. The armed goons and their blonde master hadn't disturbed much on their way through.

Scarlet slammed a palm on one arm of her chair. The chair slowed down, then resumed its previous speed.

Bryan moved to walk next to her. "Are you okay?"

The Expedition, Inc. hacker blushed. "I'm fine. It's fine."

Bryan stared at her. "That wasn't very convincing." He put a big hand on her shoulder. "Scarlet?"

She brought her chair to a halt. Bryan looked ahead at Jason, Niles, and Sofia. A short, clipped whistle brought them all to a halt.

Scarlet sighed. "Okay. I'm okay. Really." She blushed, meeting the big man's eyes. "Thanks." The console on the arm of her chair she had been accosting beeped and flashed yellow.

Jason joined them. "What's up?"

Scarlet sighed. "Battery is low."

Jason clucked. "Damn." He checked his watch. "I didn't realize we'd been down here so long."

"Time flies when you're underground, running from armed bad guys," the hacker quipped.

Bryan frowned. "What does that mean? Should I carry you?"

Scarlet made a choked noise. "What? No." She blushed. Bryan blushed. Jason groaned.

"We gotta go," Sofia interrupted from the door leading out of the command center. "That door is thick, but those beams won't hold forever."

Scarlet nodded. "Okay." She didn't look at either man next to her as she guided her chair toward the waiting Sofia. A few taps on the two control panels at the ends of each arm put her chair into low-power mode. LiDAR mapping, disabled; headlights and other features, disabled. Jason and Bryan fell in next to her without a word.

Jason looked over his shoulder. "Niles, come on!" The portly academic put his phone away and trotted toward the group. So much history in these rooms.

They reached the ramp up to the security foyer. The sound of people ramming a metal door in between shooting at it was still audible, but barely.

Even though most of the doorways didn't have doors, they closed any they found behind them as they made their way into the long corridor that connected the security foyer to the ramp to the armory level above.

"So, what now?" Niles wondered.

"We get to the surface. Call for help," Jason said.

"Just like that?" Sofia asked from the head of their little procession.

Jason shrugged.

Niles chimed in, "We know they have that door that leads, presumably, out of the bunker."

"The door the bad guys came in through," Scarlet offered.

"Well, yes," Niles admitted. "Surely there isn't an endless stream of malcontents coming through that door." He looked around. "Right?"

No one replied.

"Seriously, there can't be that many of them, right?"

Bryan picked up his train of thought. "We know the tunnel we came in through wasn't what they were using. Right?"

"Right," Jason agreed.

Sofia smiled. "And we," she pointed to Niles, "found the tunnel they use to get things out of the airport and this bunker."

"Well, the door, anyway," Niles corrected.

"So, there's at least one other tunnel we haven't seen," Bryan said.

No one spoke until Sofia said, "Shit. That tracks." She continued, "That storeroom is going to be guarded. Those guys back there, they're pros. Their friends will be too."

"The other tunnel has to be in that room," Niles added. "We must have missed it."

Sofia nodded. "You're right. The door we came through was still sealed. They're only using that one room."

Jason shrugged. "There we go. A plan."

"That's not a plan," Bryan said.

Jason smiled. "It's an 'us' plan."

Clark and his team reached the end of the tunnel. He was next to the makeshift door, listening to people talk on the other side. Whoever it was, they were professional enough to keep their voices down.

He looked at this team, making a series of hand gestures. All six nodded, moving their assault rifles to ready position as quietly as possible.

Clark removed two fist sized cylinders from a pouch on his thigh. He pushed against the metal panel that served as the door, easing it open as far as he dared. He pressed the activators on both devices, counted to ten, and tossed them into the room beyond.

The low conversations stopped immediately, followed by shouts of surprise, then two loud pops and bright flashes of light.

Clark pushed as hard as he could against the door, making room for his team to stream in, shouting orders to stand down. Bullets started to fly.

The men in the storeroom were definitely professionals. To a man, they took a knee the moment the flash bangs went off.

The moment the first crack of gunfire registered, Clark's team took up positions at the ends of the aisles of shelves, taking high and low stances. They couldn't see any better than their opponents, so the first few minutes were mostly random shots meant to keep the other side off balance.

As the smoke drifted into the other storeroom and through the makeshift door that led to the plains, the gunfire became more targeted.

Two of the smugglers went down. A third took a bullet to his thigh. The wound was bad. Blood was pooling around him. In a haze, he grabbed a grenade and hurled it toward the source of energy gunfire.

"Grenade!" someone shouted.

Clark swore and dove through a doorway. The woman, Taylor, leaped through after him a split second before an explosion rang everyone's bells and brought several tons of cinder block and bedrock raining into the storeroom.

Clark rolled on his back and opened his eyes. The air was thick with dust. Breathing felt like ingesting small pebbles.

"Sir?" Taylor coughed.

"I'm good," he rasped. "Report!" he shouted as loud as his dust covered throat would allow.

Groans and coughs were the only answer. The area was darker than before. The little sticky light that was in the room must have been damaged or buried. Who throws a fucking grenade in an enclosed space?

With a groan of his own, Clark got to his feet. He felt around for the flashlight he hadn't needed until now. Clicking it on, the beam went only a foot or two before being swallowed by the dust cloud.

"SPS, call out!" he croaked.

"Ramirez," someone said off to the right.

"Ballinger," another voice called out.

That was it. A few others groaned. He couldn't tell if they were his people or the enemy.

He turned to the woman near him. "Taylor, check them." She nodded. He moved deeper into the room where the smugglers had been during the gun fight.

One corner of the room was a ruin of shelving, concrete, dirt, and rock. A door on the back wall, a door that didn't match its surroundings, was knocked half off its hinges. A pair of boots stuck out from under the small landslide. A body was just visible under a crumpled piece of shelving.

A man a few feet from the door groaned. He was mumbling something about wine. Clark kneeled down to check him for injuries and weapons. Finding nothing serious of the former and none of the latter, he zip-tied the man's hands and stood.

"Sir," Taylor called.

Clark looked around, spotting two more bodies. He joined Taylor and two men. Both were bruised and beaten but otherwise still mission capable. He nodded to both.

One of them, Ballinger, inclined his head toward the entrance to the tunnel. "Sir."

Clark turned. "Shit." The entry was collapsed. A pile of rubble was almost waist high. It didn't look like clearing the rubble would be impossible, but it would take time.

"You three good to continue the mission?" Clark asked. He got three curt nods. "Good. We'll either leave through their door or clear this when we get back." He motioned to a door leading deeper into the facility.

This place was really getting on his nerves.

Sofia held up a hand, balled into a fist. The group was in the spiraling ramp that led up from the long security foyer. The sound of gunfire echoed into the chamber.

"Oh, great. Another gun fight," Niles said from the middle of the group, next to Scarlet.

"Pretty far up there," Bryan said. Sofia nodded.

Sofia looked at Jason, eyebrow arched.

He shrugged. "Only way out, is up."

She sighed and resumed her slow march up and around the ramp to the armory level.

The armory was exactly as Jason and the others left it, same with the foyer beyond it. The gunfire was somewhere ahead, and that meant it was in either the research room they were approaching or one of the storerooms.

An explosion rocked the ramp, sending cracks spider webbing around the cylindrical chamber and through the ramp itself.

After the rumble of the explosion died down, the snap-popping of splitting concrete continued.

"We should hurry," Bryan urged.

They resumed their march up the ramp, those in the rear going only as fast as Scarlet's chair would allow, which at this point was about the pace of Jason's grandmother's walking speed. The chair had been losing power and speed gradually since leaving the command and residential level.

Scarlet, Jason, and Bryan rounded the last bend, the arched doorway to the research room visible. A loud pop filled the space a second before the floor tilted.

Bryan lunged forward, his fingers just catching a seam in the concrete ramp that wasn't there before. He looked over his shoulder as Jason and Scarlet slid around the bend out of sight.

The rumbling stopped. From above, Sofia shouted, "Jason! Scarlet!"

Bryan shouted, "I'm fine, thanks!"

"Where are the others?"

"They slid around the bend." Bryan swung himself up and around in order to get both hands on the edge he was clinging to.

"We're fine!" shouted Jason.

"One casualty!" Scarlet added from the darkness.

Bryan looked up through the dust to Sofia and Niles. Both shrugged.

"What does that mean?" Sofia asked.

"Her chair. It's toast," Jason called back.

Scarlet looked down at her lap. One of the larger drive wheels was sitting cockeyed relative to the chair body. One of the smaller directional wheels was completely snapped off. She sighed. "This sucks."

Jason nodded as he looked around. They had fallen into a crevasse about five feet wide. It was a miracle neither had been seriously hurt. The ramp floor had given out; likely a water leak or groundwater somewhere had eroded the soil under it. The explosion's concussive force had been the weakened cement's last straw.

Scarlet and her chair had bounced against the walls before hitting the solid floor. Jason fell next to her.

He looked up. They weren't that deep, maybe five feet. He could certainly jump and grasp the lip. That didn't solve the bigger problem. What to do with Scarlet? She couldn't jump, and he wouldn't be able to with her on his back. "We're gonna need a hand and a rope," he called.

"Wait one," Sofia called back.

Scarlet began rummaging through the pockets on the sides of her chair, sliding things into pockets on her pants and shirt. She tapped on the right-hand control panel. It blinked a few times, but that was it. She swore.

"What's wrong?" Jason kneeled next to her.

"I liked this chair," she whispered.

Jason nodded. "Yeah."

A rope slid off the ledge above, landing next to the pair. "Coming down," Bryan said from above, a moment before he eased over the top.

He landed in a crouch. "Air Osborne, ready for departure." He grinned. A makeshift rope harness was strung across his broad torso.

"Uh," Scarlet said.

"Oh, for crying out loud," Jason grated. "You two can work out this angsty attraction thing on the move." He reached under Scarlet, easing her out of her chair.

Scarlet made an enraged squeak but otherwise said nothing. Jason hitched his head to the side, indicating Bryan should turn around.

Jason gently eased Scarlet's legs through the loops at Bryan's side. The harness wouldn't be comfortable but seemed well made. Scarlet slid each arm through a loop at the big man's shoulders, then around his thick neck.

"Not so tight," he croaked.

"Oh, God, so sorry," Scarlet said with a gasp, loosening her grip.

"Kidding. Hold as tight as you like."

Jason looked at the ceiling. "Serenity now."

"What's that, Jace?" Scarlet asked.

"Nothing. Let's go."

Bryan led the way, climbing up the length of rope with ease.

CHAPTER 12

Chasing the intruders back toward the airport, Elizabeth Murphy was scowling. Another team should have arrived by now, waiting in the store room. They'd meet up with that team and take these annoyances out. It wouldn't matter in the end, but it should feel good.

Chloe was not going to be happy. This operation had been running smoothly for years. It was all a shambles now. Her friend and boss would have to make an example of someone.

Elizabeth had been in Washington, DC, grooming a young staffer at the Pentagon to turn him into an asset when the drunk young man mentioned seeing a memo about a facility built in the 1980s. It was out in Colorado and used their airport construction as cover. He was in such a hurry to impress the beautiful woman that had approached him at the bar that he told her everything he knew.

It wasn't much, but hearing that an underground

facility that almost no one knew about existed and was just sitting unused set the wheels in motion. After excusing herself, she set off on a research project that ended up spanning several months.

Chloe had sent people to check on her more than once during that time, afraid she'd taken up drugs or one of the other illicit vices that the organization peddled.

By the time she came before the council of Dragons, she was armed with a partial list of companies involved in the project, several top military officers and advisers that she believed to be connected, and a list of Colorado locals she thought she could turn.

Finding people she could leverage was a specialty of hers, a specialty the Ten Dragons made use of often. Whether it took days or weeks, once she set her sights on someone, they rarely escaped her grasp.

The council approved the first phase of her ambitious project. Outside the council, Chloe had expressed her pride at her friend coming up with such a novel new way to increase the syndicate's business.

Tracking down the often-retired construction workers had been a challenge. Many had moved after retirement without providing a forwarding address. Several had gone off the grid when the first wave of climate refugees had flooded into Colorado and other interior states.

Once she had someone who knew where the facility was, digging the tunnel to it had taken almost a year, working at night, forging work orders and organizations frequently. To make sure that getting goods out of the facility was as easy as possible, the tunnel had to be dug with a shallow grade, which meant that it ended a half kilometer from the facility itself.

Erecting the small concrete radio tower facility over the top of the tunnel had been easier than expected but still an exercise in municipal juggling. Keeping airport and city authorities busy had taken a lot of Elizabeth's time back then.

Once the tunnel was dug and she had shown that after accessing the topmost level of the underground facility, they could gain access to the airport through an excavation of their own undertaking, her superiors had granted her the funds and resources to move forward on the next steps.

Finding the right people within the airport's management and services layers had been another minor challenge. Installing a door that wouldn't show up on official records, and ensuring no one noticed, was a task she relished executing.

The final piece of the project was the mules. Murphy herself had personally recruited nearly half a dozen airport employers to move cargo for her. Each thought themselves the sole victim of her blackmail and extortion. When one got brave, or stupid, she had them eliminated and found another.

Chloe had been reluctant on the matter, wanting to insert known Dragon operators into the airport. Elizabeth had argued that it would take too long to get their people into the right positions.

She had argued that leveraging existing employees would be more cost-effective. They would know less, and have more to lose should they be discovered, and would be more easily replaceable. Best of all, they were in the positions they needed to be in already.

It had worked. For years. The smuggling operation had been one of the most profitable arms of Chloe's part of the syndicate. Coordinating the shipments took some extra work; ensuring that no two deliveries overlapped required finesse, but it worked.

The cargo annex expansion had seemed innocuous enough that she hadn't been overly concerned about it when the news broke. Now she regretted that decision. She hoped that it wouldn't cost her her life.

Even if her people could eliminate every one of these trespassers, she realized the facility's existence was known and the airport would send more people to explore this find. There was simply no way this operation could continue. Denver, as a smuggling route, was burned.

Jason and Bryan helped each other up and around the bend in the ramp toward the research space and the rest of the team. Bryan went through the opening first, Jason on his heels.

Bright flashlights clicked on, blinding the three new arrivals.

"Stop right there," a familiar voice said.

Despite the low light provided by the scattered stick-ems, three powerful flashlight beams were pointed right into the faces of Jason and the team. From behind his outstretched hand, he spotted Niles and Sofia standing to the side, arms raised. He looked at Bryan, who was shielding his eyes.

"You mind?" Jason asked.

The lights clicked off one at a time.

Clark Haggerty looked directly at Bryan. "Mr. Osborne, report. What happened to Jacoby?"

Bryan tried to stand straight, but Scarlet's weight forced him to hunch forward a bit. He coughed. "I'm not sure, sir. We became separated, and the last we saw, he was heading back up the tunnel."

Haggerty nodded once. "He's dead. Executed."

"I knew it," Sofia said, a bit too proudly.

Haggerty spun. "He was a good man."

Sofia didn't back down. "He was stupid. More concerned with making you happy than getting any type of answers. Looks like he paid the price. Hope you're happy."

Before she could react, the big ex-Marine's fist impacted her nose, snapping her head back. In a single fluid motion, she turned her stunned stagger backward into a pivot that gave her the momentum to strike out with a side kick that caught Haggerty in the midsection.

"Stop it, you two!" Jason barked.

The two ex-military brawlers backed apart, glaring daggers at each other.

Haggerty stepped back one more step, then motioned to his two colleagues. "Take them into custody."

"The hell?" Scarlet said from Bryan's back.

"What?" Niles stammered.

"Like hell," Sofia growled.

The two haggard-looking security contractors moved to

flank Jason and the team. Bryan stood awkwardly watching his colleagues and his new sorta-friends. He could feel Scarlet's heart racing against his back.

Jason shook his head. "The hell are you doing, Haggerty? You don't have any jurisdiction down here."

"Or any right," Scarlet said, smacking her palm on Bryan's shoulder. The man winced. "Sorry," she whispered.

Bryan cleared his throat. "Sir, they didn't—"

"Shut the fuck up, Osborne." Haggerty turned to his subordinate. "You and Jacoby had one job." He pointed to Jason. "Keep them from fucking this operation up. If that cargo expansion ..." He threw his hands up. "Now you're a fucking sherpa for this cripple?"

No one saw it coming. Bryan's hands wrapped around Haggerty's throat in the space between two heartbeats.

The entire research area erupted in pandemonium. The two SPS officers were shouting at Bryan. Haggerty was trying to shout. Jason, Niles, and Sofia were shouting at the two SPS officers. Scarlet was shouting at Bryan. What few guns were left were all out and pointed at people.

Niles stepped into the middle of the shouting, both hands out, patting the air. "Please, everyone, calm down." He turned to Clark. "Mr. Haggerty, this facility is a piece of unknown history. A government-installed bunker to ensure continuity in disaster. This place has historical value beyond, well, anything you can comprehend. Certainly more than a simple expansion of an airport cargo facility."

The big man spun. "Do I look like I care? This whole whatever-it-is can wait. SPS has a financial duty to ensure the airport remains profitable, and completing the cargo annex is how that happens." He waved a hand. "I don't give a flying fig about whatever museum you think will care about this. If I get my way, we'll dump a few thousand tons of concrete down here and move on."

Jason raised his hand. "You don't under—" Haggerty lunged towards him, punching him in the face. The sudden savage attack caused everyone in the room to gasp.

Sofia sprang into action, throwing an elbow into the face of the woman next to her before lunging at Haggerty.

The big man was fast, but she was faster. Shoving Jason aside, she landed a right hook on her opponent's left cheek. Before he finished his stumble, her left hand was coming for a jab. Haggerty was momentarily stunned by the ex-Marine's attack. It was enough for her to knock him backward with a side kick before squaring off again, her face a rictus of rage.

Jason caught himself, turning to the nearest security man and tackling him. He landed three blows on the man's midsection before the much bigger man heaved Jason up and off him.

Jason landed with enough force to knock the wind out of him. He looked up to see a bolt of blue energy slam into the man about to kick him. The big man twitched as a look of confusion crossed his face. He looked at his hands, shaking them slightly. Bryan came into view, punching the man in the jaw.

It was enough distraction for Jason to roll over and get his feet under him. He shouted, "Cut the crap!"

Everyone stopped moving.

Bryan stepped forward, Scarlet holding her stunner out in front of him. "Is this the best use of our time?"

Haggerty opened his mouth, but bullets struck the ceiling, stopping whatever words were forming. A stick-em exploded, showering sparks everywhere.

Shouting was coming from the ramp. More bullets flew through the arched doorway, forcing everyone to back away from the entry.

"Form up!" Clark Haggerty shouted. He motioned to two of his officers, then to one side of the room. He directed Jason and the team to the opposite side.

Bryan stood watching the two groups seek shelter, unsure which way to go. He finally chose, moving to join Haggerty, despite Scarlet's protests.

Bullets struck the ceiling, sending chips of concrete raining down.

Jason and Sofia hefted one of the stainless-steel tables over onto its side, the shiny top providing better cover. Niles, crouched next to them, shouted, "This started out so fun."

Sofia grinned, her teeth still pink from the blood from her nose. "You're not having fun?"

From behind them, the voice of Clark Haggerty shouted, "Fall back!"

Niles grunted. "I stand corrected. That man can say intelligent things." He crawled on his hands and knees from the work table he was sharing with Jason and Sofia to the table Bryan was crouched behind.

Bryan nodded to the heavyset man. Inexplicably, the dark-skinned college professor was still in his blazer despite being covered in sweat and dust. The big man shrugged. "Ready?" He felt Scarlet's grip around his neck tighten. She was ready. The academic nodded. Bryan stood up enough to squeeze off a few shots, forcing their pursuers to pause. The pair scrambled toward the next work table.

Scarlet leaned close to Bryan's ear. "If we get out of this. You're taking me to dinner." He nearly stumbled. "If we die, I'll haunt your spirit."

"Is it possible for one ghost to haunt another?" He got them behind a work bench. The stairs to the storeroom complex were visible.

"Let's not find out." She pulled herself forward and kissed his cheek.

The big blond man tensed. "We're gonna make it," he ground through clenched teeth. Scarlet chuckled.

A bullet flew close enough overhead that both of them winced. The blonde woman and her strike team were on both sides of the doorway to the ramp, taking turns, leaning out to fire. Even with Haggerty and his two officers, the balance of power was not in their favor.

Jason, Sofia, and Niles joined Bryan and Scarlet. At a work table a few feet away, Haggerty and his people crouched. "Now what?" Jason shouted.

The running gun fight made its way up the ramp from the security level up to the research room.

Reaching the research space, Niles turned to the others. "What now?"

"We get back to the storeroom," Sofia answered. "The collapse did not fully block the door these assholes were using to get out."

"The collapse?" Jason repeated.

"Not fully blocked?" Niles added.

Bryan shrugged, stood, and opened fire. He didn't wait, turning and scrambling to the next piece of cover.

Everyone crawled and crab-walked after him, before the enemy gunfire resumed.

Oracle was beginning to lose hope that she'd figure out what her friends were up to when she saw a memo appear on the system. It was on the servers that handled business affairs.

A quick scan revealed that the current security contract was to be ended. The firm's employees had on more than one occasion jeopardized the financial footing of the airport, as well as the lives and well-being of its employees. Additionally, several people had been killed as a result of decisions made by this sole actor.

None of that sounded good, for that employee at least. The memo further referenced independent contractors. That had to be the Expedition, Inc. team.

She made a decision. The security department servers would have to be breached.

The remaining SPS team and Jason and the others made it to the steps that led up to the storeroom complex.

He turned to Haggerty. "What's the situation up there?"

The other man looked as if he wasn't going to answer, then said, "One of theirs tossed a grenade. Took out four of mine and most of theirs. There are two alive and cuffed. The grenade collapsed the roof in the larger storeroom, the one they were using."

Sofia rubbed her face and swore. Niles ignored her, saying, "You found their airport access, though?"

Haggerty nodded. "I don't think it was damaged."

"You don't think?" Jason pressed.

"We were in a hurry. We didn't check it, but the ceiling on that side of the room was intact. So..." He spread his hands.

Sofia rose and squeezed off a few shots. "Still seven pissed off smuggler criminal types over there. They're in the room and spreading out."

"We can't stay here," Bryan said. His forehead was bleeding, and one eye was swollen closed. Jason wasn't sure when that happened. Scarlet, still tied to his back, looked none the worse for the wear, all things considered.

Jason reached over and tapped Niles' shoulder. "Go."

One by one, the team funneled into the first storeroom, the one full of canned peaches.

"This is the dumbest possible way to die! Surrounded by expired canned fruit," Sofia shouted over the gunfire.

"I like peaches," Niles quipped before wiping his brow.

Jason looked at Sofia. "We could die being eaten by red pandas."

From Bryan's back, Scarlet scoffed. "I think it'd be worse to die being slowly crushed in the bottom of a bucket gradually filling with hot dogs." Everyone turned. She shrugged. "What?"

"That's so incredibly disturbing," Sofia said.

"And specific," Bryan agreed.

"Very," Niles added.

Jason made a face. "Hot dogs?"

Haggerty scowled. "God damned amateurs."

Sofia rolled her eyes.

The gunfire behind them had stopped. Jason motioned everyone back. He grabbed a can off the nearest shelf. Olives. He tossed the can, letting it bounce down the stairs. "Fire in the hole!" he shouted. They could hear the people below scramble. He turned. "Come on!" He didn't wait, running toward the door that connected this room to the next, the one repurposed by the smugglers—the room that was either their way out or a dead end.

"Did you just throw a can of sardines like a grenade?" one of Haggerty's officers asked. The short woman.

Jason shrugged. "Olives. It worked, didn't it?" He motioned everyone through the hatch.

Inside the second storeroom, Sofia let out a low whistle. "Damn, you all did a number on this place."

The other SPS officer, a young guy with dark brown hair and eyes, said, "It wasn't us."

Sofia shrugged. "We're gonna have to hurry." She pointed at the half-buried security door she, Niles, and Matt had found. It was half open and barely hanging on its last remaining hinge. The ceiling collapse had done a number on the room and the more recently constructed — and by the look of it, less well constructed—access tunnel that led off to the east.

Haggerty moved to the opposite wall. "Here." He pulled a metal panel aside.

"Woah," Scarlet said.

Bryan nodded. "So many tunnels."

Niles leaned in to examine the tunnel. "Looks intact."

"You're running out of places to go," a crisp British voice called out. "Just give up."

"Fuck you!" Haggerty shouted.

Jason rubbed his face. "Really?"

"What?"

Jason sighed. He motioned the group to come closer. "We should split up."

"Wha—" Haggerty started.

Sofia silenced him with a gesture.

Jason continued. "No time to argue. Bryan, you take Scar and Niles and head to the airport. We'll see where the other tunnel leads. I'm thinking they'll follow us."

"Sir, he has a point," one of the men, Ballinger, said. "We can draw them off, let the others get back to their terminal, and let the airport PD and everyone else know what's going on."

Haggerty nodded. "Fine."

"Cute trick," the British woman shouted from outside the storeroom.

The group broke and headed for their respective tunnels. Sofia shoved Bryan into the tunnel. "Get moving. You'll be the slowest." The big man opened his mouth to argue, but a shift in Scarlet's grasp around his neck and shoulders killed the argument. He headed in. Sofia shoved Niles next. "Be careful." The big man nodded and hustled after Bryan and Scarlet.

Sofia joined Jason and the SPS team. "Time to go," she whispered.

Jason looked around. Spotting what he was looking, for he said, "Go. I'll be right behind you."

"Jace..." Sofia said.

He waved. "Go." He turned to Haggerty and his remaining officers. "Go!"

As one, the SPS team and Sofia nodded and scrambled over the rubble into the tunnel.

Jason kneeled down next to a body. It was in black. Why hired goons always had to wear black fatigues was beyond him. He patted the body down, brushing enough rubble and debris away until he found the man's thigh pouch.

Empty. Damnit. He pulled his pistol and fired two shots into the connecting doorway. The muffled orders he heard confirmed that the British woman and her team were just outside—no longer afraid of canned food.

He scanned around. Found another body, this one a woman, probably one of Haggerty's, based on the accessories. Her thigh pouch had what he was looking for. His hand closed on two familiar cylindrical shapes.

Gunfire roared into the room. Two black-clad men rushed in, each moving to one side of the doorway. He fired two shots before darting toward the smuggling tunnel.

"There!" a woman's voice shouted.

He didn't slow or look over his shoulder. Bullets impacted the cinderblocks over his head. He dove into the tunnel, dropping both cylinders.

He stumbled once but kept his footing, counting in his head. A bullet struck the metal railway next to his foot a moment before two loud pops filled the tunnel with light and sound.

CHAPTER 13

Stepping out into a well-lit concrete box, Scarlet, Niles and Bryan looked around. The big man with Scarlet on his back whistled. "Smart."

"What's that?" Niles asked, pulling the door closed.

Bryan gestured to the space they were in. "This is possibly the remotest corner of the cargo and luggage facility. I can see why their setup worked so well." He turned to look at the door. "That doesn't look out of place, and since it locks from the inside, any curious airport worker wouldn't be able to sneak a peek."

Scarlet grunted. "If I never see another shelf full of crap, it'll be too soon."

Niles fished out his mobile phone. "Do we know the number for that project manager? Melissa, if I recall correctly."

Bryan snatched the phone, tapping the screen. He tapped a series of buttons before raising the phone to his ear. "Hi. This is Officer Osborne, SPS. Put me through to

Ms. Jackson. I understand, but she'll want to hear my report immediately."

The trio walked toward the elevators while Bryan waited.

Finally, he said, "Ms. Jackson, this is Officer Osborne. Yes, one of Commander Haggerty's people. I was in the underground...bunker...thing. I'm in the lower cargo and baggage area now...Yes, we came in through their secret tunnel. The rest of the team, including Commander Haggerty, took another tunnel. Yes...Yes, ma'am, we assume the other tunnel will exit into whatever facility the smugglers...sorry, yes, smugglers, are using as the final stop for their goods."

The elevator doors parted.

"Yes, ma'am. We're on our way up to the main level. Okay, see you there." He hung up. "That woman has a colorful vocabulary. I think we're going to get the brunt of it shortly."

He was not wrong. The elevator doors slid apart a minute or two later, bringing them face to face with a six-foot-plus, dark-skinned executive in a charcoal gray suit. Behind her, a much smaller and paler woman stood.

Before the trio even exited the elevator car, Latricia Jackson said, "Explain. Now."

Bryan opened his mouth but stopped short when Scarlet put a hand on his shoulder. To the side, he heard Niles take a deep breath.

Niles explained, at some length, the last day's adventures, his theories on the smugglers, and his views on the historical value of the contents of the structure and the structure itself.

Finally, the airport Chief Executive held up a hand, stopping further explanation. "Okay. What now?"

This time, Scarlet was the first to answer. "We need to send whatever backup we can to wherever Jace and Sofia are likely to come out. They've got seven angry and better-armed crime army guys on their tails."

"Crime army?" Jackson repeated, her brown eyes locked on Scarlet's.

"You got a better name?"

Melissa Rafferty, who had been silent so far, said, "We can get airport PD up out of the construction site. But where do we send them?"

The five of them stared at each other until Scarlet made a whooping noise and slapped Bryan on the shoulder.

"Ow."

"Sorry." She waved her hand. "Niles, gimme your phone."

"What, where's yours?" the portly academic replied, clutching his phone.

"In my chair, at the bottom of a hole, in a hole." She snapped her fingers. "Gimme." He did. She tapped on the screen a few times, then said, "Let's get out to the private hangar. Have your police types meet us wherever you have the *Peregrine* parked."

Melissa and Latricia looked at each other, each mouthing the word, *Peregrine*.

Seeing that, Scarlet said, "Our plane."

"Oh," Melissa replied. "You named it?"

"She names everything," Niles offered.

An exasperated Latricia Jackson said, "Do we have time for this?" Everyone shook their heads. "Then let's get the fuck going." She turned on her heel and walked toward the nearest exit. "Melissa! Make sure a car is waiting for us," she barked.

Melissa looked up from her phone. "Already on it."

After the police and fire personnel rounded up the would-be thieves and ensured no one else was around, they departed, leaving Oracle to her mission.

She had broken through the SPS firewalls and was examining everything she could find when a message arrived via her satellite uplink.

Launch Emmet. Search east of airport. Looking for smuggler exfil.

Oracle did not know what Scarlet was referring to but did as requested. The cover of *Emmet*'s docking bay slid open. With a whir, the drone lifted from the fuselage of the *Peregrine* and departed.

Accessing the hangar's systems, she opened the large doors and powered up the *Peregrine*'s engines.

Another message came in.

Prep for take-off.

"This tunnel could use some improvements," Sofia quipped. She was at the head of the small procession that was running down the smuggler tunnel as fast as they could, away from the airport. They knew it was only a matter of minutes before their pursuers entered the tunnel and had an unobstructed firing line on them.

"Where the hell are we going?" one of the SPS officers asked from the rear of the group.

"Forward," Clark Haggerty growled.

A pair of loud pops echoed through the tunnel.

"What was that?" another of the SPS people shouted.

"Flashbangs, I think," Sofia replied. "Faster!" She increased her pace. Under her breath, she added, "Jason, you better not be dead. I don't know your password to the payroll system."

Up ahead, Sofia spotted the tunnel floor sloping up. "Come on!" she urged.

From behind the group came a shout. "What are you all doing here? Move it!"

Unlike the bunker facility and the airport, the end of the tunnel that Sofia burst through had no door or anything else covering it. She ran up out of the packed dirt and concrete tunnel into a room not unlike the one they left underground: cinderblock construction, shelving lining three of the walls, with a few free-standing units in the middle of the room.

Clark and his people emerged, fanning out, followed shortly by Jason. Clark turned to him. "That your work? The flashbangs?"

Jason nodded. "Thought it might buy us some time and cover our trail." He shrugged. "Even a little."

The big man nodded. "Smart." He turned away, missing Jason's wide-eyed expression at the maybe-a-compliment. "Ramirez and Taylor, go see where we are. There must be a door somewhere." The two officers nodded. He turned to the last of his people. "Ballinger, cover the tunnel."

The man nodded.

Jason looked around. "Damn."

The group was in a concrete building that looked like it measured fifty feet to a side. The tunnel opening was near the rear wall of the building, sloping down and under the wall. The only other feature of the space was the wall opposite the tunnel, with a single door in it.

Taylor and Ramirez reached the door, opening it. "Looks like a reception area," the former shouted.

Before any further exploration could occur, the sound of voices came from the tunnel. Before the man, Ballinger, could react, his body jerked as bullets ripped into him.

"Down!" Haggerty shouted as he scrambled toward the nearest set of shelves, his gun held out behind him, squeezing off shots randomly.

Jason and Sofia got behind a shelf. The former looked at the tunnel opening as two black-clad warriors emerged and ran for cover as they fired. He looked at Sofia, holding up his pistol. "I'm out."

She looked around. Nodding, she stood, fired two shots, and reached up onto the shelf above them. "Here." She offered him an assault rifle. "Don't shoot your face off."

Jason looked at the gun, then her. "Where'd you get this?"

She fired, striking one of their opponents. By then, all seven had emerged from the tunnel mouth. Bullets were ringing off the metal shelving and chipping the concrete walls. "Shelf of guns, right above the boxes of coffee that probably isn't coffee."

Jason examined the gun. Sofia usually insisted he stick to pistols. A bullet struck the shelf overhead. Jason stood and squeezed the trigger.

Two more black-clad troopers fell amid screams before Jason's rifle clicked empty. Sofia grabbed him, pulling him toward the door at the front of the building. Haggerty and his people were on either side, firing into the room.

Something made a loud pop behind them.

Bullets shredded the drywall that separated the two spaces, forcing everyone to the ground. The small SPS woman, Taylor, had the front door open. "This way!" She waved.

From somewhere inside the larger storage area at the rear of the building, smoke was billowing.

Reaching Taylor and the door, Sofia looked over her shoulder. "You started a fire."

Jason frowned. "How do you know it was me?"

Sofia's expression was all the answer he needed.

The other SPS officer, Ramirez, slammed the

connecting door closed before ducking toward the door to the outside. Bullets shredded the interior door.

"Blondie is mad," Sofia said. She looked around. Clark and his people were crouching behind a black SUV, weapons pointed at the door to the building.

Joining them, Jason looked around, then up. "A radio station?"

Clark grunted. "Good cover. No one would wonder about vehicles coming and going at all hours to check on things. Far enough from the airport that my teams never noticed it at all."

Jason frowned, sensing the admiration in the man's voice. He expected a few types of emotional responses from the big military contractor. Admiration wasn't on the list.

Gunfire brought his attention back to the door to the fake radio station building. Wishing he'd grabbed a clip for the rifle Sofia handed him, he crouched while the others returned fire.

By now, smoke was billowing out the small windows along the top of the walls just under the almost flat roof.

Amid a lull in the gunfire, the British woman seized her opportunity. "We're coming out!"

"To surrender?" Jason called out.

"To talk!"

"About your surrender?" Jason replied. Clark elbowed him in the side.

The remaining black-clad mercenaries and their well-dressed—and remarkably, still mostly dust-free—boss stepped out. There were four smuggler goons left.

"How is she not filthy?" Sofia whispered. Jason looked at her. She was covered in dust and sweat, the two forming a paste on her face and clothing. He shrugged, assuming he looked the same.

The British woman smiled. "Well, isn't this a fine how-do-you-do?" She pointed to the SUV Jason and the others were behind. "Looks like there's a car for each side. Why don't we just each get in one and drive away?"

Jason looked at the others, then said, "Uh...because you're criminals and we're not."

The other woman clucked. "This operation is burnt. Let us leave. You'll never see us again. You've got that whole underground whatsit to explore." She beamed. "I can make it worth your while."

Jason opened his mouth but was cut off by Clark Haggerty shouting, "Do tell."

Everyone turned to the big man. He shrugged.

"What're you doing?" Jason hissed.

"Exploring options." There was no trace of humor or guile in the man's reply.

The small SPS woman, Taylor, gaped.

"So, all that *mierda* you spouted about the airport's bottom line, having a job to do, blah blah blah?" Sofia waved her free hand.

Seeing her moment, Elizabeth Murphy pressed forward. "You all have proven your resourcefulness today. In my line of work, resourcefulness has value. There's room in our organization for people such as yourselves."

For a long moment, Jace, Sofia, Haggerty, and his

people remained where they were, silent. Then Haggerty stood.

His subordinates, Taylor and Ramirez, tried to pull him back down, but he shrugged them off. Stepping around the front of the vehicle, putting himself fully in the line of fire, he said, "I'm interested."

"You asshole." Taylor stood. Her head snapped back. When her body struck the ground, there was a single bullet hole between her eyes.

"Everyone is free to make their own decisions," Murphy said, lowering her pistol.

Jason and Sofia exchanged a look, the latter shrugging. "She's a good shot."

Jason made a face.

Haggerty strode confidently toward the criminal syndicate team. Several assault weapons followed him toward the British woman.

Ramirez tore his gaze away from his fallen colleague, turning to Sofia and Jason. "What do we do?"

Jason shook his head. "I'm working on it."

"Work faster," the other man hissed.

Jason made a face. "I don't even know you."

Sofia shoved both men, hushing them. She pointed up. Jason raised an eyebrow, unsure of what she was trying to get across.

Then he heard it. A low whine. A familiar low whine.

He mouthed the word, *drone*. Sofia nodded.

Ramirez shook his head and mouthed, *What?*

Aboard the *Peregrine*, Scarlet, now in a loaner courtesy wheelchair with the airport's logo stenciled on both sides, pointed to the screen before her. "There."

The sleek black aircraft was sitting out in the open on the tarmac, ready to take off. It was standing room only in the crew compartment, and as many airport police as could fit were jammed in the lounge. In the cockpit, Scarlet was at her station. Bryan was standing over her. Latricia Jackson and Melissa Rafferty were hovering near the workstation opposite Scarlet's.

Niles was in the pilot's seat.

The whine of the electric engines grew in pitch as the plane rose from the ground.

"Who's flying this?" Jackson demanded, turning to look at Niles, who threw both hands into the air.

The *Peregrine* continued to rise.

Melissa moved to look over Niles' shoulder at the controls. "Is someone remote flying this thing?" She met Niles' eyes, the older man shrugging.

"Something like that," Scarlet said, not looking up from her station.

"Is that safe?"

The airport Chief Executive waved a hand. "Forget that. Is it legal?" She looked at Melissa. "Make a note."

Ignoring the banter, Scarlet said, "We'll be there in a few minutes." She pointed at the display. "Looks like a radio station tower or something." She finally looked up, meeting Latricia Jackson's gaze.

The plane rotated once it was precisely fifty feet above the tarmac and headed off to the east of the airport.

Through the forward windscreen, a faint black smudge was rising into the evening sky.

Jackson crossed the small cockpit. Then the plane tilted a bit, forcing her to reach out, clutching Bryan's arm. Not letting go, she looked over Scarlet's shoulder. "Well, shit. I approved that thing. Like, a couple of years back, I think." She jabbed a free hand at the screen. "That's where these smugglers were based out of?"

Niles turned to look at the two women and said, "I suspect it isn't a base of operations. Too risky."

"Too small and exposed," Bryan offered.

The woman looked at him, frowning. Realizing she was still gripping his bicep, she looked at her hand, then up at him. "My..."

The big man blushed.

Scarlet took her attention from the screen. "He's mine. Get your own."

Jackson released her grip, pulling a face. "Okay, girl." She smiled.

Bryan coughed, pointing out the forward window. "Look."

They were much closer now. Flames had nearly engulfed the low building next to a radio tower. A small group of people was standing around outside, near two black SUVs.

CHAPTER 14

Haggerty and the blonde woman were speaking too quietly to be heard by Jason and the others. Sofia was fuming, her eyes glued on the security-contractor-apparently-turned-criminal-employee. The blonde's goons were keeping their weapons trained on Jason and the others.

A throaty electric roar replaced the whine of the drone hovering overhead. The deep thrum of two powerful electric engines.

"They're gonna kill us," Ramirez insisted.

Jason shrugged. "I mean, they'll try."

The other man just stared at him. "You're unarmed. Her gun is empty, and I have like three rounds left." He held his small submachine gun up.

Jason clucked. "I have a round or two." He sighed and pointed in the direction of the growing whine. "Cavalry is on the way. Just need to wait."

The other man turned and squinted into the deepening dark. The inferno next to them was ruining everyone's night vision. "Cavalry?"

By the time Haggerty and the criminals noticed the inbound plane and raised their weapons, the *Peregrine* was roaring overhead, her external lights blinding them. Bullets pinged off the underside of the plane as it passed overhead, churning up a cloud of dust.

Sofia didn't miss a beat. The moment everyone's eyes were on the matte black aircraft buzzing them, she was sprinting, closing the gap between her and Clark Haggerty.

Jason slapped Ramirez's shoulder. "That's our queue." He rose.

"To what? Die?"

Haggerty turned just in time to see Sofia lean in to tackle him.

Jason smirked and bolted toward the knot of criminals. He couldn't let Sofia do this on her own. He hoped the plane landed soon—and full of Marines. He fired two rounds at the nearest mercenary before his rifle clicked empty. Thankfully, that man hit the ground.

Just behind him, Ramirez followed suit, firing at the knot of armed goons. Another man fell.

The remaining criminal goons turned from watching Sofia and Haggerty battling it out to see Jason and a larger man rushing toward them. As the second man fell to Ramirez's fire, one of them shouted a warning that was cut off by Jason's shoulder impacting his midsection. The two hit the ground, rolling.

"All your talk, and in the end, you're a goddamned sellout," Sofia growled, circling slowly.

She and Haggerty had gotten some distance, each already sporting a swollen eye or broken lip. Or both.

The big man jabbed, then leaned into a spin kick. The latter caught Sofia a glancing blow as she pivoted to avoid the punch.

Sofia rolled her shoulders, dancing from side to side, her eyes glued to Haggerty's. She feinted a jab, letting him raise both arms to form a shield. In the span of a heartbeat, she changed her punch to a roundhouse that caught the bigger man on the chin, sending him staggering.

Jason's fight was going less well. He caught his opponent by surprise, but that lasted only a few seconds. After kicking Jason off of him, the bigger and more muscular man lashed out with a roundhouse followed fluidly by a backhand chop that sent Jason staggering away, almost falling to the ground. "You can't slap people!" he shouted, holding his cheek.

Jason took a deep breath and rolled his shoulders, doing his best to channel Sofia. He moved in fast, hoping to catch his opponent by surprise, striking with two quick jabs to the man's midsection. One was blocked, and the other landed, sending his opponent staggering backward.

Murphy gestured to her people, those not engaged in combat, catching their attention. She pointed to the nearest SUV.

"Live to fight another day," she whispered, opening the passenger door as one of her men ran around to the driver's door.

The SUV's tires spun as it roared away from the

building and fire. Just as Elizabeth Murphy thought she might get away, a matte black aircraft lowered itself right in front of the vehicle. There was no room for the driver to maneuver. The SUV crashed into the plane's nose.

The *Peregrine* sat down a hundred yards from the ruined SUV. The boarding ramp descended, disgorging almost a dozen airport police officers who quickly moved to encircle the SUV.

Bryan, pushing Scarlet, Niles, and two angry airport executives, cautiously followed.

The two fistfights ended when all parties were surrounded by shouting police with weapons drawn.

Haggerty had pinned Sofia. He was about to land a punch when he looked up and swore. Sofia pushed him off and got to her feet. "*Pinche cabrón,*" she spat.

Bryan did his best to push Scarlet over the uneven prairie. He was on the heels of Latricia Jackson, with Melissa Rafferty hot on his own heels. Niles was trudging along behind them all.

The airport's CEO reached the assemblage of international smugglers and paid adventurers. She looked at the dirt- and dust-covered group until her gaze settled on Clark Haggerty. "Explain."

The big man looked around, then opened his mouth. Sofia cut in. "This *maldito pendejo* was going to take a job from British Barbie over there." She jabbed a finger toward Haggerty.

Latricia's and Melissa's mouths both fell open. The former regained her composure first. "Clark?"

The big man opened his mouth, but Jason cut him off, offering a detailed retelling of the events over the last few hours, ending with Haggerty taking the blonde woman up on an offer of employment. SPS Officer Ramirez corroborated the entire story.

Latricia stood silent, one finger absently tapping her chin. Finally, she inhaled and turned to Clark Haggerty. "Consider this official notice that SPS's contract is terminated, effective immediately."

"Fuck you."

She leaned in. "Fuck you!" She gestured to one of the airport PD officers. "Get this asshole out of my sight."

The man nodded, reaching for Clark's shoulder. "Sir..."

Haggerty flinched his arm away from the other man's grasp. He scowled at Jason and Sofia, then Latricia and Melissa. He stormed off out of the circle of law enforcement.

Latricia looked at the officer she spoke to a moment ago, nodding that he should follow Clark.

By this time, a few pickups and a van, all with airport PD decals, had rolled up to the scene. Haggerty was escorted to the van.

"*Puta*," Sofia said to the departing man's back.

With Haggerty taken care of, all eyes turned to the British woman, now handcuffed along with her remaining goons.

Jason looked around, finding Niles, Scarlet, and Bryan. "Good to see you three. Thanks for bringing the cavalry."

Bryan nodded. Scarlet said, "We couldn't leave you two high and dry." She winked at Sofia.

The Expedition, Inc. team and airport personnel watched as a firetruck made its way up the dirt access road; news helicopters could be seen in the sky off in the distance.

Latricia looked around, then clapped her hands. "Listen up, people!" Everyone nearby stopped and turned. She nodded to the airport PD chief. "Chief, let's get these folks back to the airport and into holding cells. I'd like to speak with the blonde when we get back." The man nodded.

He was about to turn and issue orders when Jackson continued, "Have two of your people escort Haggerty and other SPS officers off the property. We'll work out their property later. They aren't setting foot in the building. Get them in their cars and on their way." When it was clear she was done addressing him, the chief issued orders, and his small police force went into action.

Melissa Rafferty cleared her throat. "We should all get back to the airport before they arrive." She pointed to now much closer helicopters. "Let's not give them any more than we can until we're ready."

Everyone nodded. Jason said, "The *Peregrine* will get us back to the airport fast, and the choppers won't even see her." He smiled at Scarlet. "Right?"

As Bryan pushed her around a large rock, she said, "Yeah. I mean if they had active radar, we'd be in trouble."

She pointed to the nose of the plane, dented and missing paint in several places. "Fender bender."

Once everyone was back at the airport, Latricia Jackson's priority was assuring the media, the mayor of Denver, and the FAA that there was nothing wrong with the airport and that everything was under control.

After availing themselves of the small restroom aboard the *Peregrine* to get cleaned up, Melissa escorted the team to a conference room in the administrative area, providing drinks and food from the food court in the terminal. In acknowledgment of their roles, Bryan and Officer Ramirez were allowed to remain on airport property with the Expedition, Inc. team.

There weren't many SPS officers left in the building, and they were rounded up and escorted to the employee parking garage. The airport police called in every able body they could to take up the slack while things were in flux.

Two hours later, Melissa and Latricia walked into the conference room. The latter said, "Well, this is certainly a shit show." She took a seat at the head of the table. "I spoke with your British friend. Apparently, in exchange for protection, she's willing to spill her guts."

"Really?" Jason leaned forward.

"You thought she'd be all, 'I'll die with what I know'?" Jackson said. Jason nodded.

"Ma'am, what happened to Commander Haggerty?" Ramirez asked.

Jackson frowned. "He and the rest of SPS have been escorted from the property. Once we're done here, you two will be as well." Ramirez frowned and looked down at what was left of his meal.

Niles raised his hand. "What did the woman say?"

Melissa answered. "Not much. She confirmed that her organization built the radio tower and tunnel into the airport. She said she'd share more when the FBI arrived. They'll be here in a few minutes, actually. Denver office."

Niles nodded. "Interesting."

Jackson frowned. "I know you gave me the high-level explanation earlier." She looked at Niles, Scarlet, then Bryan. "How about a bit more explanation on what the hell all this is and, more importantly, how I unfuck this whole thing?"

Jason and Niles took turns explaining what the facility below the airport was. Scarlet and Sofia added color commentary where they could.

Bryan filled in a few parts where he could, and Ramirez filled in the gaps toward the end around Haggerty's incursion into the facility.

Jackson shook her head. "When those cargo movers came forward with their tale, I shoulda made sure they were kept under wraps. Haggerty must have found out about them."

"One of our people always monitors the security office," Ramirez confirmed.

An assistant came in with a tray of beers. Everyone

grabbed one.

Cracking open her beer, Jackson said, "So, let me make sure I have it. The blonde and her organization set all this up. The fake radio station building. Found someone to excavate a tunnel into the bunker and then to the airport. Bribed or threatened people to connect the bunker to the airport. Found other employees to leverage for the day-to-day smuggling." She looked around the room. Everyone was nodding slowly.

Scarlet nodded. "Yup. Sucks it was something so pedestrian. I was really hoping for an Illuminati compound."

Jackson shook her head slowly. "Conspiracy groupies," she said to herself. "All of this to smuggle things through the airport, intercepting them before they were processed by customs."

"That sums it up." Niles nodded.

Jason turned to Melissa Rafferty, sitting next to Sofia. "Sorry to say, your project is likely scrubbed."

She sighed. "Yeah, kinda figured." She turned to her boss. "I'll get JK's team on it, see what we can salvage, maybe look—"

The executive waved a hand. "Forget that. You're gonna be busy managing the shit show that this is going to become when the government shows up."

Niles cocked his head. "The government?"

Jackson nodded. "It's their bunker."

Head nods and tilts all around the table.

Jason said, "All things being equal, this may prove more lucrative to the airport than a new cargo annex.

Museums the world over will clamor for artifacts from the inside. The government may have built it, but they built it here, under the airport. I'm guessing it's yours now. Could make for a profitable attraction."

Jackson smiled. "I like the way you think. I know that technically, your job here is done, but I get the impression you and your team would be invaluable in navigating the next several weeks."

Jason nodded. "We'd be happy to stick around. I can get an addendum to our contract sent over in the morning." He looked at his watch. "Uh, later today."

After that, everyone agreed to turn in and regroup after they were more rested. The FBI would be busy for a while anyway.

A week later, the cargo expansion project was officially on hold while they drew new plans up that would move the annex a kilometer north of the originally proposed location. From what Niles and Jason had determined, that would keep all construction well clear of the bunker. It would, however, require closing a runway from time to time. It was the best compromise Melissa Rafferty's people could come up with. Latricia Jackson had spent two full days negotiating with the airlines that would be affected.

In order to keep as many of his people working as possible, JK Scheinberg assigned some of his best excavation teams to digging out the two tunnels that connected to the old bunker. They found no new booby traps.

The moment there was a big enough opening in the rubble, Niles and Jason lead a team back into the bunker to begin cataloging as much as they could.

Jason worked out a finders' fee with the airport, since selling the find to a museum was out of the question. Jackson had been more than happy to find a compromise as, true to Jason's assumption, the airport was fielding calls from museums all over the country.

Until she could free it from its deep underground tomb, Scarlet was forced to use a loaner and decidedly low-tech wheelchair. After she was done outfitting it with pouches for tablets and other bits of tech, it was uncertain whether the airport would get it back.

To Jason's amusement, Bryan, the big SPS officer, was still around, despite every other warm body attached to the mercenary-for-hire contractor having been escorted from the property and told to never return. He made himself useful as muscle when not pushing Scarlet around the airport.

Jason learned that since Haggerty hadn't actually committed a crime or even accepted a job with the British woman, no charges could be filed. It was a minor consolation that SPS was facing several lawsuits from the airport as well as the families of every officer that died during "the bunker job," as Scarlet had dubbed it.

Deep in the bunker, Jason found Niles in what they had dubbed "Camp Mole Town." He was at the large planning table with a map of the country on it, flipping through a file folder he had found. "Hey, old man."

The portly academic had several notebooks lying open

across the tabletop and a pencil clutched in his mouth as he thumbed through the decades-old papers.

Niles turned. "Oh, Jason, hello! How did the tour with Ms. Rafferty go?"

Jason shrugged. "So far so good. Sounds like she's got a firm grasp on the Army Corps of Engineers guy. She'll have two teams down here tomorrow, two more in a week. They'll get to work reinforcing things, making sure it's safe."

"Good, good," Niles replied, his attention already back to his task.

Jason smiled. He could see the spark in his friend's eyes as he poured over whatever was in the files arrayed before him. He opened his mouth but stopped when Sofia came in from the command center area.

"Hey, Prof. Lunch time." She stepped through the doorway with two brown bags in her hands. She looked at Jason. "Sorry, Jace, didn't know you were here." She shrugged, holding out one bag for Niles.

Jason smiled. "No worries. I gotta get back up topside."

Scarlet was sitting in the airport courtesy wheelchair across from a small table in the food court of the C Terminal. She had spent days exploring each terminal to find the best food. C Terminal had won. It was also newer, having been renovated fifteen or so years ago. The all-access badges the airport gave the team made getting around easy.

Across the table, Bryan smiled. He hadn't left her side

in a week. His excuse was that she needed someone to push the chair while she did whatever she did on her tablets. No one bought it. No one challenged it.

"So," the big blond man said.

"So," Scarlet replied.

"I'm thinking deep dish pizza and the new Meow Wolf exhibit. I hear they—"

She interrupted with a wave of her hand, slurping a mouthful of spicy noodles. "Yes, please."

He nodded. "I'll make reservations."

She grinned. "So, what're you gonna do next? I mean, it sounds like SPS isn't gonna be around long."

The news was running nonstop stories about the military contractor and the fall from grace of one of its shining stars. Of Clark Haggerty, nothing was being said and he hadn't been seen since driving away from the airport more than a week ago.

Bryan shrugged. "I dunno. Plenty of SPSs out there. Someone is always looking for ex-military."

She smiled. "I'm sure something will pan out."

That night Jason, Sofia, and Niles watched the oddly matched but happy couple exit the light rail platform at Union Station, heading toward their first stop of the night.

As the trio headed off toward their own destination, the delicious restaurant Scarlet had introduced them to— the one tucked in an alley that smelled like urine—Jason smiled and asked, "Still planning to leave us?"

Sofia stopped dead in her tracks. "What?" Her head snapped to the side to glare at the academic.

Niles flushed, his skin taking on a darker hue. "Jason!"

Jason put both hands up, palms out. "You had plenty of time." He smiled innocently.

Sofia squinted. "Explain, *abuelo*."

Niles spluttered. "Over drinks?"

Sofia maintained her squint, then said, "Fine."

Jason followed the two of them into the grand lobby hall and toward the Terminal Bar at the far end of the building from them. They had time before their reservation.

Passing a combination coffee shop and ice cream parlor, he thought to himself that now they had two criminal and criminal-adjacent people to watch out for: Phillipe Bouchard and Clark Haggerty.

Not to mention whatever organization the blonde woman worked for. The FBI agents had kept that to themselves, rushing the blonde and her people to an undisclosed location.

Sofia took a seat at a long wooden table while Niles went to the window to place their drink order. Jason sat down next to her. He already knew what Niles was going to say. He knew the moment he saw his friend's eyes down in the bunker earlier.

Tonight was for enjoying his friends. Everything else was a problem for another day.

The End

I hope you enjoyed this first adventure of Jason and the Expedition, Inc. Team. I'm excited to see where in the world they find their next adventure! I hope you'll come along!

Reviews are the lifeblood of indie authors. If you could take a minute to leave a review, it'd mean the world to me. Don't know what to say? "I liked it." Is a perfectly fine review to leave.

Did I mention how much social proof is worth to indie authors? :)

OFFER

As they say, there's no harm in asking, so here we go.

If you can help connect me with someone who can get Expedition Inc. on a screen (Big or Little) I'll cut you in for 10% (Up to $10,000) of whatever advance is paid.

Send me an email and we can discuss.
rights@johnwilker.com